Here's what they're saying about:

TERROR
Before the Dawn

"The Big Thompson Flood was the worst disaster in Colorado history. Bertie Woodward gives the event a human scale that we haven't seen in print before, and describes how people actually had to deal with the realities, moment to moment."

—Phil Walker, Radio Broadcast Personality
Author of "Modern Visions Along The Poudre Valley"

"Bertie Woodward reveals one woman's silver lining in the cloud that wreaked havoc and suffering for so many who experienced the 1976 Big Thompson Flood in *Terror Before the Dawn*. The characters undergo and express a range of emotions as they are touched by the disaster: fear, loss, compassion and hope. And as some lives are torn apart, others are spared and united. Set against the backdrop of northern Colorado's peaks and canyons, Woodward's storytelling explores the heart's terrain."

—Tom Katsimpalis, Curator of Interpretation
Loveland Museum/Gallery

"This story is not only an e⋯iting romance, but a gripping account of a natura⋯
—Mary Hagan, Member C⋯
Ro⋯

continued...

"A daringly romantic story about the resilience of life and love in the face of tragedy."
   —Debra Benton, Benton Management Resources, Author of "How To Think Like A CEO."

"A gripping tale of love and faith - one woman's struggle through tragedy, silence and loneliness that will leave you wondering...'Could I have done that?'"
   —Janice Geist, Owner, Sunstone Marketing President, Centennial Pens & Publishers

"I've lived in this area for many years, and of course have heard many stories about the Big Thompson flood. But this "fictional romance" is the most exciting and terrifying tale about that disaster I have seen. The human events and the superhuman efforts of volunteers and rescuers, victims and survivors are carefully created, and the logistical information of rescue operations cleanly comes from the story. This is local history at its very best, encapsulated into a romantic story of a hero and wise survivor of the canyon tragedy."
   —Ellen Eagleson, Owner, Jade Creek Books Fort Collins, Colorado

TERROR
Before the Dawn

by Bertie Woodward

To Rosaline,
Best wishes to the
reader!
Bertie

TwinStar
PUBLISHING

ISBN: 0-9709169-0-6
Published by Twin Star Publishing
Fort Collins, Colorado
First Printing: 2001

PRINTED IN THE UNITED STATES OF AMERICA

TERROR Before the Dawn
CONTENTS

Acknowledgements
Dedication
Big Thompson Canyon Location Map
Author's Note
Photo of Big Thompson Memorial

Bibliography
About the Author
ADDITIONAL BOOKS ORDER FORM

Acknowledgements

Steve Sweek
Creative Writing instructor at Front Range Community College

Writer's Group Teammates
John Calhoun
Dave Arns
Donna Wichelman
Carol Andersen
Miriam Hampton

Arlene Albrandt
Don Edmondson

Critiquers:
Mike Bjarko, Ink & Scribe
Marlene Depler
Phyllis Woodward

Marketing Advisor
Ceil Higgins

Book Packaging
Becky Asmussen, Image Graphics

Illustrations
Tom Peacock, Becky Asmussen

Photography
Katie Asmussen

Dr. Dorothy Abbey
Who graciously shared her impressions of those early days
while volunteering at the rescue center.

Others who have read and have had the courage to comment!

Dedication

To my husband, Russell, who continued
to encourage me in this project
and to Aunt Lucille, who made the publishing
seem in the realm of possibility.

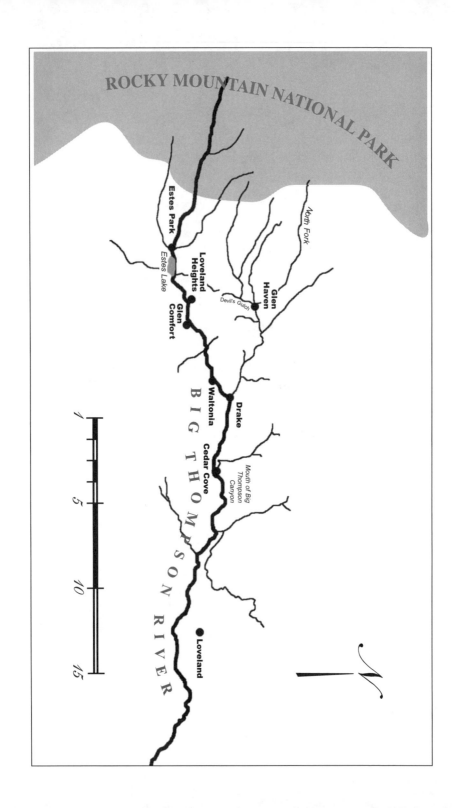

Author's Note

"It has never been my intent to tell the personal stories of the survivors and their families. They lived it and I did not. Although there may be some illustrations that allude in similarity to actual events, these accounts have been fictionalized lest they cause concern to those who were present at the time.

While researching the events that took place on that fateful night, the human interest of the tragedy compelled me to want to tell the story in a fictional romance.

My prayer is that those who survived the tragedy have found life more precious because they have had a second chance at life!"

—Bertie Woodward

Chapter 1

Friendships

Karyn's face registered disappointment. Sitting in her condo living room with her feet tucked under her, she balanced the telephone on her shoulder. She flipped the rafting brochure in her hand while listening intently to Jim's voice on the line.

"I'm really sorry that it won't work out for me to go rafting down the Poudre River with you on Saturday." Seated at his desk in Secure Investment's office building, Jim stared at his appointment calendar lying open in front of him. Thumping a pen on the arm of his leather chair, he said, "I have a special client flying in from Chicago on that day, and we haven't been able to arrange another time. Can you get Cindy to go with you since we've already made our reservations?"

Her brow creased in a frown. Karyn replied, "I guess I can call her, but she didn't sound too excited about it when I told her you and I made plans to go."

"Hey, Beautiful, I'm really sorry it's worked out this way. You know how much I've looked forward to the trip. You just go and have fun without me. Okay? I've gotta go, but I'll talk to you later."

Karyn hung up the phone and pulled her dark hair into a

1

ponytail, then dialed her best friend's number. *Why would Jim make another appointment when we scheduled this months in advance?*

"Cindy, what are your plans for Saturday?" Karyn asked, holding her breath, waiting for a reply.

"Nothing special. What did you have in mind? I thought you and Jim were going rafting."

"We were, but he had to cancel because of an important meeting. How would you like to go with me?"

"Karyn, you know I'm not terribly excited about that kind of water sport. Maybe if I were a better swimmer, I'd get more of a charge out of it." Cindy looked out at the foothills from her apartment window in Loveland. "Not only that, but the Poudre will be high after the rainy season, and that doesn't exactly thrill me."

"Cindy, you know the guides are experienced, and you don't have to worry about being thrown overboard. Oh, come on. It'll be fun and a new experience for both of us."

"Let me think about it and get back to you," answered Cindy.

"I have to confirm our reservations sometime today. That doesn't give you much time to think about it. Why don't you just say yes right now and save yourself the trouble?"

"Okay, but I may never forgive you for talking me into it!"

"I'll risk it," said Karyn as she hung up the phone. An amused smile crossed her classic features. Cindy had been her special friend all through high school in the Chicago suburb of Bloomingdale. They had shared all the mutual activities of school proms, dating, and job experiences.

Karyn recalled the day Cindy had moved to Loveland, following a broken engagement a month prior to her wedding date. Crushed from the shock, she had come to Fort Collins to spend a two-week vacation with Karyn. After looking into the job market, she decided to stay and work for a Loveland publishing company. It had been a year since the move.

Smiling, Karyn thought about her friendship with both Jim

2

and Cindy. For some reason, Cindy had taken an immediate dislike to Jim. "He's such an egotist and so cocky about his good looks," was her comment when questioned about it.

Jim had also come from the Chicago area. He and Karyn first met in a speech class at CSU and struck up a friendship. Their relationship was purely platonic, and both seemed satisfied to leave it that way, even though they had been dating steadily for the past six months. Karyn had no illusions about the fact that although Jim was fun to date, he was poor husband material. I could never marry Jim. He's too self centered and materialistic.

Karyn's thoughts drifted as the late afternoon sun shone through the window, casting a golden reflection on the cream colored carpet. The mountains loomed on the skyline in the distance, as if beckoning her.

❖ ❖ ❖

Cindy knocked on Karyn's door at seven o'clock. When Karyn opened the door, Cindy greeted her with, "I can't imagine why I'm doing this. Best friends should never make this kind of request. Why did I let you talk me into this?"

"Let's discuss that another time. Right now, we'd better be on our way, or we'll be late. If you don't have fun today, I promise I'll never ask you to do something like this again. Is it a deal?"

Smiling with a mischievous grin, Cindy put her hands on her hips saying, "I'll hold you to that forever." Karyn picked up her tote bag, heavy with a camera and her sunscreen. Laughing, they walked out the door arm in arm.

❖ ❖ ❖

Twenty people crowded onto the bus at Ted's Place, a well known landmark in the area where rafting groups gathered. The rustic log building housed a restaurant and service station, and its location made an ideal meeting place for those headed up Poudre Canyon.

3

Lush, green alfalfa fields spread out along the roadside until they reached the base of the foothills. As the bus rambled across a noisy cattle guard, the driver shouted, "Now you know you're at the entrance to Poudre Canyon." Those familiar with the canyon laughed, and the tourists looked puzzled.

Cattle grazed along the side of the road, looking up as the bus passed, but they were so accustomed to the traffic that they claimed the right-of-way. The gently sloping hillsides were scattered with sagebrush, yucca, and early spring flowers. Willow trees grew in clusters along the river's edge. Mountain homes dotted the pine-covered slopes, some rustic and others more contemporary.

"Wouldn't it be fun to own a home like that one tucked away in the trees," said Karyn, as she admired a multi-level home clinging to a rocky slope and partially concealed by timber.

"Dreamer. We're lucky just to be this close to the mountains," added Cindy, looking up at the jagged rock formations on the right. "I'm so glad you talked me into coming to Colorado."

A jovial, laughing group disembarked at the drop site for rafters. Donning life jackets, they stood for the last minute instructions from the guides before climbing into rafts at a quiet spot in the river.

Randy, the guide, had the physique of a body builder. He assured the novices that he was an experienced rafter, and others in the group were equally capable. "For those of you who have never been rafting before, we'll place you in the middle of the raft. Just keep your head about you and follow instructions as we paddle down the river. There'll be some areas of white water so be prepared when I tell you what's coming up ahead." With all the charm of a talented salesman, he said, "We want you to have a good time so that you'll be sure to come back again.

"Eric and Kevin, since you've rafted here before, sit in the center of the first boat where we need some strong paddlers. Steve, take the front, and the first four people fall in between.

Barry and Hal will be in charge of the second raft. Let's get loaded up."

It was early June and the Poudre River was high with winter run-off. This made rafting and kayaking more challenging than any other time of year. The river water sports had become a favorite pastime in the area for those who enjoyed a physical challenge.

"Oowhee!" said Cindy, as she hit the cold water to board the raft. "Karyn, I think you're nuts to suggest this." Several other timid souls nodded in agreement.

Karyn settled into a seating space near the center of the boat, with Cindy beside her.

"Enjoy the scenery while you can. When we get in the white water, you'll need to concentrate on paddling," advised Randy. Then he climbed into the rear of the boat and began to push off.

Warm sunlight and a clear blue sky greeted the rafters as they floated easily along in calm water. The muddy-brown water from the spring run-off rippled over rocks. As the river wound its way to the southeast, rust-gray cliffs rose to the east, contrasted on the south by a verdant forest. Behind them to the west, blue-hued mountains were hazy in the morning sun.

At a bend in the river, Randy shouted, "We're coming into the white-water, so keep paddling as I instructed you."

The roar of the river made it difficult to hear, even though Randy was shouting instructions to those in his raft.

"Forward paddle right."

The raft dropped over a cascading rush of water, throwing the back high into the air, causing the group to scream and shout when they dipped into a pool on the other side.

Cindy held her breath while they navigated around several large rocks. Then they dropped into the rushing water and began to swirl with the current. Everyone paddled furiously to get the boat moving forward again. Once they made it, someone shouted, "Hey, that's great!"

"Karyn, how did I ever let you talk me into this?" asked Cindy. Eric, tall and athletic, turned to flash Cindy a reassuring smile, "You're doing fine. Just keep it up."

Karyn looked into a pair of sky-blue eyes. His enthusiasm and skill for rafting was apparent. Something about him captured Karyn's interest. She had plenty of time to casually observe him during the two hours as they floated down the river. They both stole quick glances when they thought the other wasn't looking.

Randy navigated from the rear of the boat, choosing the best course in the river as they skirted around rocks and bounced over rushing swells. There were moments of sheer terror when Karyn was sure the boat would capsize while hurling over rocks in their path.

"This is a little like riding a roller-coaster," shouted Cindy. "It just happens to be closer to the ground!"

"I know. That's a ride I like better the second time around. Then I'm not so petrified with fear," responded Karyn, her knuckles white from gripping the paddles.

Other rafting groups followed at a safe distance in the river. Two kayakers waited, resting in a quiet pool near the bank, while the boats passed.

As they neared the end of the river run, smooth waters stretched out before them. The group relaxed and chatted amiably, floating along with the current.

It was noon when they reached the departure point. Eric turned to give Cindy and Karyn a hand up out of the raft. He gave Karyn a lingering gaze as he took her hand to help her to shore.

"Wait up, so I can get some pictures," said Karyn, hurrying to the bus to get her camera. Cindy was talking to Eric and Kevin when Karyn walked back to the group.

"Karyn, meet Eric and Kevin."

"Hi. Thanks for the encouragement and support on our first rafting trip," said Karyn, nodding and smiling. "Now for some photos to remember this adventure."

She snapped several pictures of Eric and Kevin, as well as Randy and the other rafters milling around.

To Eric she said, "Would you take a picture of Cindy and me? Without proof, no one will ever believe we did this."

Eric took the camera while the women backed up so the rafting group remained in the background. Snapping the picture, he said, "If you get copies, would you send me some?"

"Sure. Give me an address."

Walking to the bus and taking their original seats, Karyn and Cindy laughed while they compared notes about how frightened they were when they hit the white water.

"Did you enjoy the trip?" asked Eric, as he and Kevin took seats on the bus behind the two women.

"It was full of thrills. I can say that now that I'm safely on land," said Cindy, running a comb through her blonde hair.

"Karyn, what did you think of your first rafting trip?" Eric asked. He gave her a studied gaze while waiting for her answer.

Flashing a smile, she sensed her breath quickening, and it had nothing to do with her reply. "When we first got into the white water, I began to wonder what I was doing there. And I was the one who talked Cindy into going with me."

Laughter broke out in the group.

When they arrived at Ted's Place, Kevin turned to Eric. "Let's grab a hamburger here." Nodding in reply, Eric asked, "Would you two ladies like to join us?"

Cindy and Karyn gave each other a questioning look, and said in unison, "Why not?"

Karyn looked up several times to catch Eric watching her with obvious interest. She couldn't ignore the acceleration of her pulse.

They devoured the hamburgers, french fries, and cokes with relish. Karyn turned to Eric to ask, "Randy said you had been rafting here before? Do you live in Fort Collins?"

"No. I'm from California—on leave from the Air Force.

Kevin lives in Denver, and we were fraternity brothers while attending DU six years ago."

"What do you ladies do when you're not rafting on the Poudre?" asked Kevin.

"Karyn is attending CSU to complete her Master's degree in Art and Design, and working part time for a construction company. I'm a junior editor for Quality Publishing Company in Loveland. Rafting is not on my high priority list, but Karyn talked me into going when her friend Jim forgot and made other plans." The mock sarcasm in Cindy's voice was evident.

Everyone else roared, while Karyn turned a delicate pink shade.

Eric regarded her with amusement and a twinkle in his eye.

To cover Karyn's embarrassment, Cindy spoke up, "If it hadn't been for Karyn, you'd never have persuaded me to get on that raft."

"Oh, we'd never let two ladies as pretty as you fall into the river," said Kevin.

"Thank heavens you didn't have to worry about it!" Cindy pushed her chair away from the table. "This has been fun, and I hate to break it up, but I must get back to Loveland."

"Thanks for lunch," said Karyn, smiling at the two men.

"It was a great trip, and I plan to do it again." Eric and Kevin rose to follow the women, paid the bill and walked out the door. "Maybe we'll see you again. Oh, here's my address in California." Eric hurriedly jotted it down on the back of a stray business card and handed it to Karyn. "Don't forget to send me those pictures."

Once in the car, Cindy turned to Karyn. "Aren't you glad Jim decided not to come?" Cindy gave her a minxy smile.

"The boat trip was fun, and it was nice to meet Eric and Kevin."

"I think Eric was attracted to you. He had this certain way of looking at you. Don't tell me you didn't notice!"

"I was too busy watching Kevin flirt with you," teased Karyn. It was not hard to be attracted to Eric with his Nordic good looks, blond, wavy hair and flashing smile. "Eric's from California, and

I'll probably never see him again." But that didn't keep her from being more than a little disappointed.

During her lunch hour on Monday, Karyn dropped the film of their rafting trip off at Western Camera Shop to be developed. It was several days before she went by to pick it up. She quickly thumbed through the series of snapshots, smiling to herself while reminiscing about the trip. Her eyes lingered over the snapshot of Eric and Kevin. She could still picture Eric sitting in front of her, with muscles straining as he leaned forward paddling and laughing when they hit the white water. He radiated a masculine vitality in every move. Her thoughts brought a nagging sense of guilt when she began to compare him with Jim. Even though I like Jim, he has just never lit any fires within.

The thought echoed in her mind throughout the day, even as she climbed into bed that night. *What shall I say to Eric when I send the pictures? Why do I feel it's a big deal?*

Slipping out of bed, she went to her desk, removed some plain stationery, and jotted out a casual note. Slipping the snapshots and the note into a plain envelope, she sealed it and sighed in relief. No big deal!

❖ ❖ ❖

Eric smiled as he studied the snapshots Karyn had taken of their rafting trip. Pulling out a photo album to mount his vacation pictures, he found himself looking a second time at the snapshot of Karyn with Cindy. *Maybe I'll look up Karyn when I get back to Fort Collins.*

Chapter 2

Duty Calls

Saturday, July 31, 1976

Continental flight 567 from Sacramento to Denver was full to capacity as Eric Johnson boarded on Saturday morning. On a week's leave from Beale Air Force Base in California, he planned to meet Greg, another former college classmate, in Denver for the weekend. The two men had made arrangements to take a white-water rafting trip down the Colorado River on Monday.

The stewardess gave Eric a glance as she smiled warmly and welcomed him aboard the early morning flight. She turned for a second look as he walked down the aisle to find a seat.

After settling into his seat and stretching out his six-foot-one frame to get comfortable, Eric pulled a brochure from his carry-on bag to read about white-water rafting in Colorado. He smiled to himself in anticipation of the trip.

The stewardess went through the pre-flight instructions while some of the passengers looked bored or ignored the information. Eric observed with interest. *I wonder what would happen if this load of passengers had to use these procedures?*

The plane taxied into position and held for clearance from the tower. Eric listened to the rumble as the aircraft's engines accelerated. He could hear the motors as they reached full power before take off. The plane lifted off the runway, and circled the airfield. Eric looked out the window to see the city spread out below, for miles in every direction.

"This is your captain. We'd like to welcome you aboard our Sacramento to Denver flight.

"We'll be flying at 35,000 feet, with smooth air all the way. Our arrival time in Denver will be approximately nine fifteen. We hope you enjoy your flight and plan to fly with us again."

A stewardess interrupted Eric's preoccupation by asking, "What would you like to drink this morning?"

"Coffee, please," said Eric. He tucked the rafting flyer into his bag and took the cup of coffee. The middle-aged man next to him ask for a mixed drink. Eric couldn't help but notice the odor of alcohol already on the man's breath.

Eric looked across the aisle where a young mother struggled to entertain her two-year-old daughter. The child wriggled in her mother's arms, trying to get down from the seat. Blonde curls danced with the child's every movement. The moment her feet touched the floor of the plane, she looked up at her mother with a triumphant expression on her cherubic face. Turning to look around, the child caught Eric smiling at her. Brown eyes danced with mischief and a smile lighted her face.

The occupant of the seat next to Eric finished his drink and dropped off to sleep without exchanging a word.

Glancing at his watch, Eric noted that the plane would be arriving in Denver in approximately an hour and a half. He took a mystery novel from his carry-on bag and was soon engrossed in the suspense plot.

Clear skies over the Rocky Mountains greeted Eric when he glanced out of his window. The plane circled Stapleton Airport, providing a spectacular view of the mountain range. It sent a thrill through the California-born native. He looked forward to at least one ski trip on the Colorado slopes each winter.

The plane touched down on the tarmac with a smooth-as-silk landing, and Eric silently commended the pilot for his skill. Picking up his carry-on bag, he made his way to the front of the plane to disembark.

Greg met him on Concourse C with a "Hi, Old Buddy. It looks like the Air Force agrees with you."

"I wouldn't want to be doing anything else right now. Even after six years in the Air Force, it just gets better and better. Are we all set up for the rafting trip?"

"You haven't changed your mind have you?" asked Greg, as he gave Eric an affable slap on the back. "If you have, I've got a couple of brave guys who would like to take your place," he chided his friend. "We're all set for Monday morning. I thought we'd meet Kevin and Tom at the Green Acres Country Club for a little golf today and drive to Buena Vista to meet the rafters tomorrow. Okay with you?"

"Sounds good to me," said Eric, as they followed the signs to the baggage area.

❖ ❖ ❖

Eighteen holes later, Greg, Eric and the two fraternity brothers decided to order dinner in the dining room. It was nearly nine o'clock when the men got up from the table to leave.

Greg and Eric were coming out of the restroom near the bar when a TV newscaster interrupted the regular program to say serious flooding had been reported in the Big Thompson Canyon, between Loveland and Estes.

As they paused to listen, the news commentator continued, "Sheriff Wilson has called all local emergency personnel from Larimer County to be available for duty. Governor Lamb has been alerted that it might be necessary to call the National Guard and personnel from Lowry Air Force Base to help rescue people stranded in the canyon."

"How can that be when it's been so nice all day?" Eric questioned.

Suddenly Eric said, with a sense of urgency in his voice, "That's a night rescue mission! They have to get those stranded people out of the canyon! Greg, drive me out to the base at Lowry Air Field. They might need some volunteer pilots for that job."

"Are you crazy, man? Eric, we're going rafting, or have you forgotten?" asked Greg in a puzzled voice .

"You said you had a couple of guys who were interested in the trip. Call them up tonight. Tell them one deposit is already paid. In the meantime, let's go. I have a feeling these people are going to need some help."

Shaking his head in doubt about the sanity of his friend, Greg followed Eric's rapid pace to the car.

Chapter 3

The Warning

Karyn sat at her desk in the office of Wade Construction, reconciling cost sheets from the various construction projects with the dealer's invoices.

Jim had promise to pick her up at six for an eight o'clock barbecue at Mike and Julie Williamson's. Their friends, who lived up the Big Thompson, had built a new cabin near the little mountain community of Drake.

"And don't be late," Julie had chided, knowing Jim was not known for his punctuality.

Karyn smiled as she thought about it. She eagerly looked forward to getting out of the office early on this particular Saturday afternoon, with still time enough to get home and pack her suitcase for the weekend. It was nearly four o'clock when she stapled the cost sheets together and walked to the file cabinet to file them away.

Wade, her boss, came out of his office and handed her a page of figures and a financial form.

"Karyn, I need this financial statement completed as soon as possible on Monday. Will you be able to get to it the first thing when you come in?"

"That shouldn't be a problem."

Karyn thought about the two years she had been working for Wade. A promoter and a visionary, he had no patience with details or delays. He had built a construction business from the ground up and was successful in anticipating the trends in the commercial and housing market. Working here had given Karyn an opportunity to gain some practical experience which would look good on the resumes she had begun to send out. The job provided enough income to pay for her tuition as she completed her master's degree in Art and Design.

Occasionally her parents sent a cash gift to help with living expenses, but Karyn liked being financially independent.

❖ ❖ ❖

Jim rang the doorbell just as Karyn made a last minute check of her suitcase. Glancing around the room, she spied her Bible on the nightstand and quickly tucked it into the corner of the weekend bag.

"Hi, Beautiful," he said. Greeting her with a brotherly kiss on the cheek, he walked to the car to load her camera and suitcase in the trunk.

Karyn pulled her windbreaker from the closet and took a quick glance in the mirror to check her outfit. At the last minute, she decided to change from shorts into white slacks, topped by a navy and white knit middy blouse. *It might be cool in the mountains this evening.* Touching up her lipstick, she ran a comb through the dark hair that fell loose to her shoulders, with just enough natural wave to make care minimal. She picked up her windbreaker and a hostess gift of nuts and candy for Julie.

Jim whistled as Karyn eased into his silver Porsche, hand-washed and every detail polished. His face beamed with pride in his newest possession. He turned to wait for Karyn's reaction.

"This car is a thing of beauty," exclaimed Karyn, surveying the interior with its plush leather upholstery.

15

"What could be better than a luxury car and a beautiful woman?" His gaze slid over her in slow inspection. "You look like you just stepped out of a fashion magazine. Maybe we could get you a modeling contract, and you could help me pay for this status symbol," he quipped. The easy banter was a pattern of light, touch-and-go humor that marked their relationship.

"Don't you wish! How many years is it going to take?" Her blue eyes regarded him with open amusement.

"Oh, probably the greater part of my working life. What's the matter? Don't you like to ride in style?" asked Jim, enjoying the exchange. He squealed around the corner, tires spurting gravel on the blacktop.

Smiling, Karyn replied, "I'm not complaining since it's you making the payments." But her silent response was, overly expensive, overly luxurious, self indulgent, which sometimes caused her to question their friendship.

Blue sky was changing to gun-metal gray, covering the evening sun when they drove through Loveland, a quiet town with a population of 16,000. West of town, pine-covered foothills sloped gently to Highway 34 leading into Big Thompson Canyon. The Tackle Store on the right, the last business located west of Loveland, remained a historic landmark for many traveling through the area.

Heavy thunderclouds hung ominously over the mountains, and obscured the view when they entered the Narrows of the canyon. Sheer rock walls rose to majestic heights on both side of the road as they followed the heavy Saturday afternoon traffic weaving around the course of the river. Clear mountain water splashed over rocks, sending up white crests while flowing on its course around south Loveland to Interstate 25.

"Aren't you awed by the ruggedness of the mountains in this part of the canyon?" Not pausing for an answer, Karyn viewed the foreboding sky and said, "I've always loved the drive through here to Estes Park. The weekend should be fun with all the Centennial activities there."

She loved Estes Park, located at the upper end of the Big Thompson Canyon. It was primarily a settlement for wealthy retirees attracted to the amenities of a mountain community. Year-long planning had gone into preparations for the Centennial Celebration to take place the following day. She couldn't wait to participate in the festivities.

"By the way, did you hear a weekend forecast?" asked Karyn when she viewed the storm mounting in the west.

"Yes, and it didn't sound like the weather was going to be too great. Forecasters predicted rain and even possible flooding in the low-lying areas of the canyon. Sounds like lousy weather for a weekend of celebrating. If I had known that I wouldn't have washed and polished my car for this trip," grumbled Jim.

"I hope Mike and Julie have planned activities that take the weather into consideration. Knowing Julie, she's probably thought of everything. She's so organized," commented Karyn. She glanced at the dark clouds scudding across the sky.

"What's happening at Wade Construction?" asked Jim, as he turned to look at Karyn. "How many projects are they working on right now?"

"Our biggest undertaking is the high-rise apartment building. We're in the final stages of construction on the first high-rise and making plans for the second. Minor problems with the subcontractors kept the phone ringing all day. I tried to complete some cost sheets for Wade on the project, but finally just had to lay them aside. If it gets any busier, I'm going to have to call in some temporary help for the front office. Usually Helen, Wade's wife, comes in to help me, but she's back east visiting her mother."

"So how was your week?" asked Karyn.

"We closed the corporate account with Northern Pacific Insurance. I just completed the final paperwork today. Business is really taking off in financial services. We're closing million dollar accounts on a regular basis. I might even be able to take you out to dinner at the Broadmoor in Colorado Springs when I get my commission."

"Sounds like fun to me, but you're impossibly extravagant," said Karyn, mocking a scolding tone. "I'm just a working girl," she said, feigning a poor-me voice. Both of them burst out laughing.

Jim and Karyn exchanged comments about the day and drove into a torrential downpour. Poor visibility slowed the heavy weekend traffic as visitors continued up the twenty-five mile mountain canyon.

"I hope we get out of this storm before we get to Mike's, but I can't see that it looks a lot better up ahead," said Jim, concentrating on his driving. "We've got ten miles to go."

Karyn felt apprehension, then fear, welling up inside her. She strained to see the road. She could only imagine how difficult it was for Jim to drive as sheets of rain battered the windshield.

The heavy traffic crept along as each driver followed the pace of the vehicle in front. Suddenly, red taillights glowed in the gathering dusk, and Jim slammed on the brakes. Traffic was stalled in a long serpentine line up the canyon.

"We won't get to dinner on time in this weather. Just hope they save some steaks for us," complained Jim. He adjusted his rear view mirror to check the traffic behind them.

The heavy thunderclouds hovering over the mountains cast ominous shadows on the steep, rocky canyon walls. Normally, the rock formations, interspersed with ponderosa pines, bitterbrush, chokecherry and rabbitbrush created scenic beauty. Today the weather conditions permitted little opportunity to enjoy the splendor of the area.

"It really did get dark in a hurry," said Karyn. "I don't like the looks of this storm. It isn't letting up at all." She felt the first cold fingers of dread steal upon her.

Lightning flashed in the distance, propelled across the sky in rapid succession, appearing to come from several directions simultaneously. Thunder boomed, jarring the earth with its percussion.

"We're in for a real storm. I didn't bring my raincoat, or I'd get out and see why traffic is stalled up ahead," said Jim, impatient with the delay. He could see nothing as he tried to peer around the car in front of them.

When Jim looked into his side mirror, he saw flashing red and blue lights coming from behind. "Must be an accident ahead. A patrol car is coming behind us."

With siren wailing, the patrol car raced past them, weaving in and out of the two-lane traffic as far as they could see.

"We picked a fine night to drive up the canyon," said Jim, with a worried expression on his face. The relentless rain beat across the windshield. The wipers swished back and forth, barely keeping up with the deluge in the gathering darkness.

"Maybe we should turn on the radio and see if we can get some weather details," suggested Karyn.

Jim fumbled with the dials on the radio and found a weather station. The announcer again predicted flooding in the lower areas of the canyon. The evening newscaster continued, "On the eve of Colorado's Centennial Celebration, it is anticipated that nearly 4,000 people will be enjoying the scenic beauty of Big Thompson Canyon and participating in events scheduled for the weekend. We do want to stress that you take reasonable precautions if you are in low-lying areas."

Another patrol car approached, with sirens blaring, and pulled to a stop beside the line of cars. A patrolman in a yellow rain hat and slicker got out of his car and stood talking to the stranded drivers. When he walked up to the side of the Porsche, Jim rolled down the window.

"We've got a washout ahead, and we're trying to figure out how to get traffic turned around and headed back to Loveland. Please be patient and stay in your car with your lights on. We'll clear out the congestion as soon as we can."

When Jim opened the window, he could see the river rising rapidly up the road bank as lights from the automobiles were reflected on the rushing water. "No wonder the road is washed out. I've never seen the river this high before."

Karyn could hear the tension in Jim's voice. Shivering from the damp evening air, as well as from a sudden realization of the danger, she sensed fear sweeping through her whole being. She told herself to take a deep breath. Her mind refused to believe that the river could actually overflow its banks. Surely not!

The patrolman came running back to their car shouting, "Get to higher ground! We have a flood on our hands! There is no way to turn around. Take any provisions you have with you, and climb to higher ground." He disappeared in the rain.

Karyn and Jim looked at each other in disbelief. How could this happen? What about the lovely weekend they had planned in the mountains with friends?

Chapter 4

Panic

Families stalled on Highway 34 climbed out of their cars when the Big Thompson River began to overflow its bank. Reluctant to leave their vehicle, an older couple insisted, "It's really not that serious. We've seen floods in this canyon before." Seized with panic, a young woman shouted, "You can stay here if you want to, but I'm going up the mountain!"

"It's flooding!" shouted an off-duty policeman, shining a flashlight at the rising water. "Hear that roar? Let's get out'a here." Grabbing his wife's hand, he started up the slope.

"Mommy, Mommy," a child cried out, trying to find her mother in the darkness.

Shocked and puzzled by the conflict of opinion, several people gathered what possessions they could to be comfortable. Some grabbed picnic baskets, snacks, and beverages. Others took blankets and rain gear. Car doors slammed and flashlights blinked in the darkness while people struggled to reach safety, climbing up various routes of the steep incline.

Jim continued to watch the river rise. He made no move to leave the car. Puzzled by his reluctance, Karyn urged, "Jim, we'd better climb to higher ground."

21

"I'm going to get out and take a look at the river. I can't believe it's as bad as all that."

Snatching a flashlight from the glove compartment, Jim pulled on his windbreaker.

"Don't wait for me. Grab what you need and head up the hill. Follow those people with the flashlight."

"I don't want to go up by myself. I'll wait for you," said Karyn, giving Jim a searching look. While voicing her concern, she reached for her jacket and began putting it on.

"Just follow the people in front of us," Jim said, impatiently. "I'll pull the car closer to the mountain. The river's beginning to wash away the bank at the roadside. I'll be up as fast as I can."

"But I don't want to go—."

"Go!" shouted Jim.

A little surprised at Jim's reaction, Karyn grabbed the package of nuts and candy she had wrapped for a hostess gift. Panic and uncertainty gripped her. Should she go or stay? Deciding to heed the warning, she asked, "Do you have a blanket in the car. We might need it."

"There's a stadium blanket in the trunk. I'll get it," and he stepped out into the rain. Handing her the blanket in a plastic bag and slamming down the trunk door, he shouted, "Now get out of here! The river's rising fast and I've got to get this car moved!"

Large chunks of the riverbank crumbled and slid slowly into the raging water. Lightning flashed from all directions, blinding them for a second, and thunder jarred the earth.

A man standing by one of the cars ahead shouted, "The road's washing away! The whole things going to go!"

At that moment a woman's scream pierced the night air.

"Jim, we have to go! Forget the car!" screamed Karyn.

Jim climbed into the car and ignored Karyn's warning. At the base of the cliff, she looked back to see him trying to maneuver the car out of the line of traffic.

Karyn stumbled up the loose gravel of the roadbank, vainly trying to quell the desperation that threatened to bring her to tears. She looked to see where other climbers had gone up the steep, rocky terrain. Her legs felt like lead, unable to propel her body forward. Panic kept her reaching out for any type of handhold to move up the precipitous incline.*How can I ever make it to safety in the dark? If only I had a flashlight.*

Grabbing at trees and brush for support, Karyn slipped and fell to her knees as she tried to make her way up the rocky, muddy hillside. Jagged lightning cut glowing patterns in the sky, giving temporary relief from the darkness, but adding to the fear Karyn already felt. Raindrops beat the earth, making the night cruel, and quickly soaking Karyn to the skin. Glad for the stadium blanket in the plastic bag, she braced her foot against a rock to tuck the candy and nuts into the bag. Slipping the handle over her shoulder to free her hands, she grasped at sagebrush for support.

What is taking Jim so long? Karyn didn't dare look around for fear of plummeting to the ground below.

Glancing up, she saw a ray of light from a flashlight nodding in the darkness some distance above her. If she could only get to the light! In the dark, it was hard to find solid footing on the wet rocks and to find a way through the tangle of rocks and rabbitbrush. Branches reached out to scratch her hands. She slipped on the wet rocks and slid into the thorns of a cactus. Tears of pain and frustration blurred her eyes and rolled down her cheeks. It's no time for self-pity, she reminded herself. She reached down to see if the cactus thorns had penetrated her shoe and broken off. Relieved, she found that the thorns had only pierced her shoe.

As she climbed higher, the rain pelted her face and dripped from her hair down the back of her neck. At the crest of a grassy knoll, she turned and peered into the darkness, hoping to see or hear Jim coming up the slope.

Gripped with a sense of fear and isolation, Karyn wondered,

What should I do, Lord? Wait for Jim to come up the mountain or follow the people ahead of me? Should I go back to see why he's not coming up? Calm down and think. I'm as safe in this spot as I can be, and I'll just wait for him here. Sitting down on a rock, she pulled the blanket out to shelter her from the rain.

Hugging her knees to her chest, she shivered in her cold and wet clothing. Soon the rain saturated the blanket.

❖ ❖ ❖

Jim opened the door long enough to flash his light along the riverbank. The rushing current was gaining momentum, eating away the road base in the left lane like a hungry monster.

He had to get the car moved! There was no way he was going to leave his Porsche to the mercy of the river.

Without warning, a vehicle in the left lane ahead was swept off the road into the swiftly moving current. Several people watched in horror as the dark pickup floated by. Quickly the bystanders scrambled up the hillside.

Jim, shocked to see how serious the situation had become, jumped into his car. How could he get his car moved and out of the line of stalled vehicles?

When he tried to maneuver the Porsche around the car in front of him and the one behind, the water washed over the left traffic lane. There was not enough room to drive out from between the two cars in order to pull off onto the shoulder at the base of the hillside. The car was wedged in!

The pavement all around him began to heave. Jim's Porsche rocked and shuddered. When he tried to force the door open, the depth of water made it impossible for him to get out. Before he could open the window to climb out of the car, the entire road buckled beneath him. The car floated into the raging river. As the force of the water carried him downstream, his last conscious thought was, *I'm going to be crushed by the cars tumbling around me!*

Chapter 5

The Angry River

Saturday, 7:25 p.m.

Terrified and overwhelmed by a sense of aloneness, Karyn sat listening to the roar of the river, combined with the repeated clap of thunder. Lightning split the sky, illuminating the ebony night. As a child, she had always been frightened by lightning and thunderstorms. She recalled her mother saying, "That's only God speaking to us from the heavens. He's just reminding us that He's still there." She found that small comfort while she sat alone in the darkness.

Questions tumbled through her mind. *What happened to all the cars in front of us? There should be lights somewhere along the canyon wall. Where are the people from the other cars? Maybe they climbed up by some other route.* Her thoughts ran on like the angry river.

Suddenly, the river thundered like a freight train coming in the distance. Objects scraped and pounded as they were carried downriver. Lightning flashed, illuminating a horrifying scene. A white house floated past, followed by huge boulders, trees and propane tanks. Karyn could smell the putrid odor of gas as the huge tanks released their dangerous fumes into the air.

Just then a motor home, with lights on and figures pounding at the windows, swept swiftly by. Cars washed down the river with headlights reflected on the muddy water. Screams could be heard from within the cars when they went bobbing by. What Karyn saw below made her stomach churn. The sound of screeching metal slamming against rock sent shivers spiraling down her spine. From where she stood, the terrain blocked any view of the road directly below. A terror Karyn had never experienced seized her as she watched objects turning and churning in the force of the water. She stood transfixed, her heart thudding against her chest, watching a car bob up and down like a plastic toy, carried on by the angry river. A wave of dizziness flooded over her, followed by a feeling of nausea. Closing her eyes, she tried to erase the sight before her.

"Those poor people!" she screamed into the night. There was so much noise from the river that no one could possibly hear her. It was as if she were in a tunnel and all the sounds bounced back at her, magnified by echoes she could not identify. Her heart pounded in her chest, and Karyn felt like the world was collapsing around her. The darkness became terrifying. She could no longer sit and listen to the destruction below.

Trembling from the chill of her wet clothing, she resumed her difficult ascent to higher ground. The rain pelted her face and her breathing became labored. Her once-white canvas tennis shoes squished at every step. Reaching the crest of a small grassy knoll, she paused to catch her breath and to peer into the darkness, hoping to see or hear Jim coming up the slope. Lightning continued to flash across the sky and thunder rumbled in the distance. Tears surfaced in spite of her efforts to control them.

I'd like to sit down and cry about the whole miserable evening. Lord, what are you doing to me? What have I done to deserve this? Ashamed of her accusing thoughts, Karyn breathed a prayer that Jim would be safe, and that the Lord would give her the strength and courage to do what she had to do. A quiet peace slowly replaced the anguish that had tormented her.

Peace of mind infused her body, giving her the additional strength to keep climbing. *Other people have come up this slope. Where are they?* In the heavy cloak of darkness, she slipped on the wet grass and stumbled to her knees. Forcing herself to get up, she continued up the slope.

Gasping, her sides burning, shoulders heaving, and every muscle aching, she climbed above the rocky terrain of rabbitbrush and reached a place where the ground leveled out. In a small grassy meadow, six people sat huddled together in the rain around a fluorescent lantern. As she walked up to them without a light, her appearance startled them.

"Have you seen anyone else come up the mountain?" she asked in a tremulous voice. "My friend went back to move his car closer to the mountain, and I haven't seen him since."

Her forlorn appearance touched the mother-heart of Jill Farris. "Honey, come over here and join us. In the darkness, it may take him a while to find his way up on top. There's nothing you can do right now."

Karyn sat down beside the others, suddenly feeling bone-deep cold and weary. The frightening experience had taken its toll on all her physical resources. To be able to rest without fear of falling, and to find some human companionship, brought a welcome sense of relief.

"I'm Jill Farris, my husband, Jake, and our children, Debbie and Ron. Sara and Mack were in the car behind ours and followed us up the mountain. How did you and your friend get separated?"

"He told me to start climbing while he tried to move his car closer to the mountainside. I should have waited there for him..." Choked sobs broke from her throat as Karyn related, "But he insisted that I start climbing. I'm worried about him. He should have been here by now. When I reached a safe distance from the river, I sat down to wait for him." She pulled a wet scarf from her pocket to blow her nose and rubbed the back of her hand across her eyes to stop the flow of tears. "I saw cars floating down the river... with lights on... and people inside... and no one to help them."

Nothing could stem the flood of tears as Karyn recounted what she had seen.

"Maybe I should take a flashlight and try to signal your friend in case he's trying to locate you. If I go over the crest of the hill, he might be able to see my light," offered Jake. "I'm surprised there aren't more people coming up by now. There were a number of cars in front of us."

Jill put her arm around Karyn until she wiped her eyes and stopped sobbing. Getting as comfortable as she could, Karyn said, "I'm sorry. I'm Karyn Anderson," as she looked around at the six faces staring at her. Her stomach began to growl and she remembered she'd had nothing to eat since lunch, adding to the light-headedness beginning to creep over her. Opening the plastic bag and ripping off the gift wrap from Julie's package she said, "I've got some nuts and candy in this bag. Would anyone like some?"

The question sounded foolish in the light of all that had happened. How could she be concerned about eating when she couldn't stop worrying about what had become of Jim. *Will he finally make his way up the mountain to join us? What a relief it would be for him to find this little knot of friendly, caring people.*

"Sure," replied Jill, reaching for the box of cherry chocolates and the tin of cashews.

"Where were you going when the traffic stalled?"

"Friends up the canyon near Drake had invited Jim and me to a housewarming party to celebrate the completion of their new home. I work for the construction company that designed and built their cabin. I wonder what they are thinking by now," said

Karyn. Looking at her watch, she realized they should have been at Julie's three hours ago. Although she was fighting for control, the sobbing began afresh. The tension of the last four hours had completely exhausted her.

No one said a word while Karyn reached in her pocket for a wet handkerchief. She blew her nose and dried her eyes with the back of her hand.

" I know, Honey. It's been a horrible night for all of us. I still can't believe what happened. When the patrolman warned us to leave our cars, Jake didn't give us time to stop and think about it.

"We have a cabin up in Estes and were returning home after a day of shopping. We didn't dream we'd be spending the night on top of this mountain. It seems like the weather has conspired to change all of our plans."

Sara sat with her head buried in Mack's arms, saying nothing. The couple, in their mid-twenties, had decided to celebrate a second honeymoon at the Stanley Hotel in Estes.

"Shucks. We couldn't hardly afford to go to a place like that," said Mack, "but we thought, 'What the heck. You only live once.' We could've died down there!" He looked down at Sara, and tightened his arms around her.

"Yeah, I know," said Ron. "I just got my driver's license, and I was looking forward to taking my girl out for the first time on my own."

Debbie sat curled up next to Jill, a frightened, shivering nine-year-old. She quietly ate the nuts and candy Karyn had shared, slowly munching each morsel to make it last as long as possible.

About midnight, the rain began to diminish. The penetrating cold and dampness of the mountain air added to the discomfort of sopping wet clothing. In an effort to ease the tension of their present circumstances, Jill made an attempt at conversation. The dialogue seemed absurd in the light of the events that had transpired.

Jill stood up and swung her arms to get warm. "Jake and I decided early this morning it would be nice for the whole family to go to Fort Collins for the day. He needed a new starter for his pickup before he could make repairs. Ron wanted to look for school clothes, or he would have been serving hamburgers at McDonalds."

Debbie sat up to add, "And we all went swimming at City Park pool after we finished shopping. That was the most fun."

"This is not exactly what we had in mind when we left home this morning," remarked Jill. "The irony of it all is the fact that here I sit in the cold, soaking wet from the rain, after spending the afternoon swimming and sunning by the pool. What I wouldn't give for some of that warm afternoon sun beating down on me right now."

Karyn sat quietly with thoughts tumbling through her mind. How eagerly she had anticipated spending the weekend with friends in their new cabin. She could never have imagined her day would end like this. Her thoughts were interrupted when Jake came through the timber, his flashlight casting a nodding beam with each step. He was alone.

"I circled the area to see if there was anyone nearby, but I didn't hear or see anything. Anyone in the immediate vicinity would have seen my light. Maybe by morning we can go down to the river and take a look. I'm sorry," Jake said, seeing the disappointment registered on Karyn's face. He sat down beside the small group huddling together, comforted only by the presence of others.

Karyn passed Jake some nuts and candy, which he didn't hesitate to take. A worried expression crossed his face, but he said nothing. Conversation was difficult with so much anxiety about what was going on in the darkness far below them. There was little they could do but wait until daylight.

Occasionally someone shifted around trying to get more comfortable or got up to walk around, hoping to warm up aching limbs.

Karyn silently prayed that dawn would soon arrive, and help would come to get them off the mountain. *And, God, please send someone to give aid to people stranded in the canyon below.* In the meantime, the night dragged on and on.

Chapter 6

Peril in the Canyon

Mike and Julie waited dinner for Jim and Karyn. The other guests arrived earlier in the afternoon, and the group sat out on the deck enjoying the view.

The sky darkened and it began to rain about 6:00 p.m. "The weather forecaster predicted heavy rain in the area," said Mike, surveying the dark clouds. "Usually, we get afternoon showers, but they don't amount to much. I don't know about this one. Maybe we'll have to cook our steaks indoors."

Mike had invited his cousin, Dan Williamson, and his wife, Susan, from Kansas to spend the week with them. Friends, Sam and Linda Coxwell, drove up from Greeley. The six proved to be a compatible group, and Julie decided to invite Karyn and Jim as well. Karyn's friendliness and easygoing charm tended to minimize Jim's unconscious arrogance.

Julie found it difficult to understand Karyn's attraction to Jim, but overlooked the obvious differences in the two, and continued to include them in her circle of friends.

Karyn and Julie became acquainted during the time they worked together on plans for Mike and Julie's new home in the canyon. Wade Construction contracted the building, and Karyn made some suggestions to create more efficient working space in the kitchen. Julie, impressed with the changes Karyn suggested, quickly pointed out to Wade what a unique asset Karyn was to his business.

"It didn't do much good to remind Jim to be on time. I can't imagine what's keeping them," said Julie, her voice edged with irritation. "I bet you're all starved to death. I'll bring out the appetizers and something to drink."

Always the perfect hostess, Julie hated to keep her guests waiting. "Mike, I think you should go ahead and grill the steaks. I have the table set up indoors because of the rain. Jim and Karyn will surely be here soon. We'll cook their steaks when they get here. It's already eight forty-five."

Julie set out the potato salad, the melon fruit basket, and a huge relish plate with various dips on the red checked cloth. It was a sight to pique everyone's appetite.

"I'm really concerned about Jim and Karyn," said Julie. It's strange they haven't called to let us know why they're late."

Mike brought the plate of steaks in from the barbecue on the deck. The aroma of grilled steaks permeated the glassed-in family room. "Let's eat, everyone."

As they filled their plates, Mike commented, "Seems like the river is running high tonight. Must be a lot of rain coming down the canyon. It sounds unusually loud."

Flood waters gained momentum in the upper canyon as north and south river channels merged, and heavy rain began washing down the hillsides.

Julie was ready to serve dessert to her guest when she heard someone on a bullhorn shouting. "Mike, what's going on? Someone down on the road is on a bullhorn about something."

"Ladies, go ahead with dessert, and we'll check it out," Mike said, heading to the closet for rain gear. "Come on, you guys."

The log home was located up the hillside, some distance from the Big Thompson River, and a bridge crossed to Highway 34, on the north side of the river. As the men followed the angling road down to the bridge, the rain stung their faces like pellets. The roar from the rushing water was deafening. When the trio reached the water's edge, they found the road had washed away, leaving no access to the bridge below their house. They stood surveying the damage caused by the deluge of water coming down the river. Mike shouted to Dan and Sam as the two men walked along the eroding bank, but they could barely hear what he was saying.

The person sounding a warning on the bullhorn had disappeared, but they could readily see the danger as the gathering force of the water continued to eat away the embankment on each side of the river. Tall spruce trees, uprooted by the rushing water, fell into the mounting debris being carried downstream. The driving rain created little gullies as the water washed off the hillside, adding to the growing danger of homes located above the river.

Mike motioned the two men back up to the house with his flashlight. *Standing by a flooding river in the rain is no place to be. Where is all this water coming from? I wonder if the dam at Estes Park has broken?*

"Let's move the cars further up the hill," yelled Mike above the raging roar of the river. "Hard telling how far that bank might erode. I don't like what's coming off the hillside either. It will eventually start to wash around the cabin."

While the other two men moved their cars up closer to the cabin, Mike flashed his light around the area to see what damage might be occurring from the rain running down the side of the mountain. Rivulets of water had turned to torrents cascading down the mountainside. Making a tour around his home, he became concerned about structural damage as the water gathered force. *I'm glad I had a reputable builder, but who would have anticipated this kind of flooding?*

Although trees blocked his view, Mike could hear the crescendo of the pounding river as the men trudged through the mud to the house.

Dripping wet, the three men hung their rain gear under a covered portion of the deck. Julie met them at the door. "What took you so long? We were really getting worried."

"The flooding is serious. I'm going to call Hallmans up the canyon to see what's happening there."

The Hallmans owned a cabin on the river a mile west of Mike and Julie's. They had been like grandparents to the young couple when Mike and Julie first started vacationing in the canyon. Mike and Julie had inquired about renting property to park their small camping trailer on during the summer, and the Hallmans had graciously consented to allow them to park it on a corner of their property.

When Mike picked up the telephone, the line was dead. "We don't have any phone service," he exclaimed. "I'm going down to look at the river again. There were some large objects floating down, and I'm not sure what they were. Honey, I don't want to alarm you, but there is a lot of water coming off the side of the mountain. Keep your eye on what's happening around the cabin. We may need to go to higher ground. Pack a lunch, water and some emergency items, just in case. I'm afraid this is serious."

The women looked at Mike in shocked disbelief before turning to stare at one another.

"I'll go with you, Mike," said Dan. "Sam can stay here in case the women need any help."

"Sounds like a good idea," said Mike, going to the storage closet for a bigger flashlight and a lantern. Struggling into ponchos, boots and rain hats once again, Mike and Dan started slipping and sliding down the hill.

When they approached the river, Dan shouted, "Looks like a car hung up by the bridge. Mike, have you got any rope?"

"I'll run back and get it while you check out the situation." Mike's voice faded as he started back-tracking up the hill.

As Dan walked to the river's edge, he heard a woman screaming for help. A Volkswagen bug, lights on, was precariously wedged between the riverbank and the bridge. Flood waters had cut a channel through the abutment to the bridge, leaving no access road to the bridge from their property. If the bridge washes away, or the debris that holds the car in place collapses, the Volkswagen is in danger of being carried down the river. In the narrow beam of his flashlight, Dan could see the terrified faces of two young women trapped inside. When Dan saw Mike's bobbing flashlight coming down the hill, he was relieved. Looking around, Dan searched for something to bridge the wash to where the women's car was lodged.

"We've got to get those women out."

Mike gasped. " That car could wash away any minute. Can we throw those women a rope?"

"What if they're too frightened to leave the car or not strong enough to fight the current?" asked Dan. "I know… Secure the rope to that tree, and I'll go out and bring them in one at a time. That downed pine there…let's wedge it into the base of the bridge on the down side in case the car starts to move or gets pushed out by all that debris."

Tugging and pulling, the two men moved the lodgepole into position and braced it between the bridge and a tree on the bank. Shedding his rain gear and tying the rope around his waist, Dan started for the water's edge as Mike secured the rope to another tree.

Dan worked his way along the debris, battling against the strong current while he fought to get near the car. The women barely had breathing space above the water level in the small vehicle. Only the debris the car rested on kept it from being completely submerged.

When Dan approached the VW, he motioned for them to roll down the window. "You'll have to come out one at a time. I can only take one of you across this trip. Who goes first?"

The fear in their eyes was apparent when they considered what would happen if the car was pushed out of position.

"You go first," said the larger of the two. "I'm a better swimmer than you are."

Dan helped the woman out through the open window and ordered, "Hang on to the rope around my waist and don't let go no matter what happens!"

While Mike stood watching, Sam came down the hill with another light. "Julie has everything under control at the house, and she insisted I come down to help you." Rapidly sizing up the pending danger, he said, "Looks like you're going to need me to help pull Dan and the woman in from the river."

Dan and the one young woman started across, while Mike and Sam struggled to keep the current from pulling the two swimmers downstream. A floating log narrowly missed them while Dan tried desperately to reach the bank. With arms aching from the effort, Mike and Sam pulled the two to safety at the river's edge.

"You'd better let me go this trip," said Mike, as he gave Dan and the woman a hand up the bank. Releasing the rope from Dan, Mike began tying it around his own waist.

The other woman was sitting on the frame of the car window, with her head up out of the water, when Mike reached the car. Debris beneath the Volkswagen had shifted, submerging the car another six inches. Mike pulled her from the window, while she clung to him in desperation. Her whole body trembled with fright.

"I've got you now. Just hang on. This river could swallow us up!"

Once they reached the shore, the two women hugged each other and wept uncontrollably. "We thought for sure we were going to drown. A wall of water hit us when we tried to move our car to higher ground," said the larger woman.

Standing on the bank shivering from the cold, the three men and two women stood aghast as a huge motor home, lights on and people pounding at the windows, was carried rapidly down the river along with the Volkswagen, the bridge, and the debris. It was agonizing to stand helplessly by and watch the tragedy taking place before them.

Both women sobbed uncontrollably. The stark reality of their own narrow escape from danger struck them in full force.

Mike stood gripping the rope hanging from his waist, feeling completely helpless. This emotion, so foreign in him, caused him to curse under his breath as he thought about the people whose lives were completely at the mercy of the raging river.

The scene of the helpless family brought tears to Dan's eyes when he thought about his own family. He finally managed to speak. "Susan decided to leave our two small youngsters with my parents in Kansas while the two of us enjoyed a week's vacation in Colorado. Am I glad they are safe at home."

Sam turned his back to the river, hoping he could erase the sight of death and destruction from his mind. "I don't know if I'll ever feel the same about this beautiful area again."

Shocked back to present reality, Mike said, "Let's get these young ladies up to the house. We all need dry clothes."

When he turned to go up the hill, a huge propane tank came downstream, spinning crazily, and hissing as it released its flammable contents. The nauseating smell hung heavily on the night air. A huge boulder tumbled down the river, narrowly missing the tank. Mike shook his head in disbelief. "Let's get out of here!" Without pausing to look back, he led the four up the hill to the cabin.

Julie ran to the door when she saw the light from the lantern as the group came up the hill. She stared open-mouthed at the two wet and bedraggled women. "What happened down there?"

"These young ladies were trying to float downstream without a boat," said Mike with a grim look.

"Oh, you poor things! Come in, and we'll get you into a hot tub and dry clothes."

"That sounds too wonderful for words," said one of them, her teeth chattering from the cold and fright.

"Mike, there's coffee and you'll find sandwiches and your dessert in the refrigerator," said Susan, as she started setting out cups. "You must be cold and hungry."

"Pack it, and we'll take it with us. We need to set up a tarp shelter near the river. What if the same thing happens to someone else? Are you guys game?" asked Mike, with a questioning look.

"We'll do what we can. It might be a long night. We probably couldn't sleep anyway," said Dan, as Sam nodded his head in agreement.

Chapter 7

Emergency Call

At eight forty-five in the evening a call came into Larimer County Sheriff's office in Fort Collins that the Big Thompson was flooding and there were rocks scattered on Highway 34, five miles into the canyon. Deputy Bob Daley drove up the road to check out the report and radioed the dispatcher in the office to confirm the caller's information. Suddenly, his voice registered panic. "We have a very serious situation here! It looks like a major flood! I need help up here to warn people in low-lying areas."

Urgent calls started coming in concerning flood conditions in the canyon about nine o'clock.

Two deputies were dispatched to assist Daley in warning residents, businesses, and campers along Highway 34.

Jeff Summers checked the river at the mouth of the canyon west of Loveland. He saw no reason for concern as he drove to the entrance of the vertical canyon walls.

"Everything looks normal in this area," he said.

The dispatcher broke in, "Bob has reported serious flooding up Highway 34, and all traffic must be diverted back to Loveland. Telephone service is disrupted somewhere between Loveland and

Estes. We haven't been able to get any information from there. Our only contact is radio communication to our vehicles."

People driving west on Highway 34 to their mountain homes were surprised to be stopped at the base of the canyon by a parked police car with flashing lights. "We have serious flooding between here and Estes," said Deputy Summers. "We are not permitting anyone past this point. You'll have to turn around and spend the night in town."

"But we have property to look after," said the first driver.

"I'm sorry, but those are my orders. We can't let anyone go beyond this point until we know just how serious the situation is." Swearing under his breath, the man turned his car around and started back down the road. Soon the others followed.

Ham operators contacted the Sheriff's office, confirming the reports of the men on patrol duty. "Extensive damage is occurring where the north and south river channels merge and are beginning to wipe out everything in their path. At the same time, the watershed coming off the mountains is causing structural damage to buildings. The rainfall has been so intense in such a short period of time, it is resulting in mass flooding."

"We have a full-blown emergency on our hands," said Sheriff Wilson as he gathered his staff around him. "A literal wall of water is coming down the canyon. We have a patrol at the mouth of the canyon and another below Estes to keep additional traffic out. We need to notify our relief agencies to come prepared: Red Cross, Salvation Army, and anyone else we might need for assistance. I'll notify the Governor in case we need to call in the National Guard. All personnel will be on immediate notice for duty, if necessary. Nothing of this magnitude has hit this area for sometime. Now get on this immediately."

Turning to his Operations Officer, he said, "I want to see you in my office. We need to coordinate these various services to have a definite plan when they arrive."

The tone of Sheriff Wilson's voice conveyed the urgency of the message. Usually a quiet-spoken man, he rarely raised his voice even under extreme pressure. His slow, easygoing manner belied the authority he possessed when the need arose. His barrel-chested, five-eleven stature conveyed the physical image of a middleweight boxer ready to go into the ring. The blue eyes were penetrating, and he readily sized up a man on brief contact. He had served as Larimer County Sheriff longer than any of his predecessors.

Brad Clark, the perfect complement for the job of Operations, stood at six-foot-two, with a massive frame that commanded immediate attention. Issuing orders came to him as easily as breathing. He wasted no time in implementing the plans for the massive task ahead of him.

Chapter 8

Safe Haven

Julie stood at the kitchen sink washing coffee cups and dessert plates from dinner when she heard voices on the deck, and someone knocked on the door. Mr. and Mrs. Hallman stood there looking frightened and forlorn.

"We just saw our cabin wash down the river," said Mrs. Hallman in a trembling voice. "We heard someone across the river warning us to get out. By the time we grabbed our valuable papers, water was coming in the kitchen door. We started up the hillside and turned to watch a large tree come down the river and crash into our house. After that it all just floated away in a matter of minutes." She gestured with her hands as if to illustrate the final collapse.

"Oh, you poor things, " said Julie as she wrapped her arms around Mary Hallman's small frame. Looking intently at John Hallman, she could see he was breathing hard and perspiration beaded his forehead. Julie was concerned about her elderly neighbor. The last thing they needed on this night, in this household, was a serious medical emergency.

"Sit down here at the kitchen table while I get you something hot to drink. Susan, would you mind checking on the young women to see if they need anything. I've made up a bed in the loft for them. They both look exhausted. By the way, we'd better not take any more baths until we find out how critical the water supply might be."

Mr. Hallman stirred cream and sugar into his coffee and asked, "Where's Mike?"

"He went down to the river with Dan and Sam. They just pulled two young women out of their car, which was hung up on our bridge. Mike thought they needed to stay down there to do what they could.

"We tried to call you earlier to see what the river looked like at your place and discovered the telephone line was out," said Julie, sitting down with a cup of coffee. "I'm so relieved you were able to find your way here in the dark."

Julie heard one of the men shouting to someone. When she looked out the window she saw someone coming up the hill with a lantern bobbing in the darkness. Walking out to the deck, she could see Dan coming to the house with six people.

Oh, no! thought Julie. *Where am I going to put all these people?* Realizing that was the least of concerns on a night like this, she extended hospitality to them in the same manner she did to her other guests.

"We're so glad to see your light. We've been stumbling around in the darkness and had no idea where we were. We're vacationing from Kansas, and the motel where we were staying went sailing down the river! We couldn't believe our eyes! We had hiked up the mountain to see if we could get some pictures of the deer feeding at dusk. When it started raining, we decided to take shelter on the porch of an empty cabin. We stayed there till the rain let up, and decided we'd better get back to the motel. As we approached, the whole thing just collapsed in a wall of water! Our van floated away with the rest of it," said the younger woman all in one breath.

"You'll have to excuse my wife for going on and on. We're still

43

in a state of shock. I'm Richard Mills, my wife Janice, my parents, James and Dolly Mills, and our two youngsters Mandy and Butch.

"We're sorry to barge in on you like this, but Dan insisted that we come up to the house," apologized the older Mr. Mills, looking somewhat embarrassed.

"Don't give it a thought," said Julie. "We're fortunate to have a house still standing! It's hard for any of us to believe what's happening on the river tonight. Linda, if you can pour these people some coffee, I'll see what I can find in the way of dry clothing."

As she went down the hall, she could hear the shocked conversation as each of her impromptu guests added something to the story of their narrow escape from danger.

"The Lord was watching over us tonight," said Mr. Mills. He looked at the somber faces around the table. "We could have washed down the river with the motel. Would you mind if I just thanked the Lord for his protection for each one of us?" he asked, reaching out to grasp his wife's hand on one side and his son's on the other. Bowing their heads, each one around the table silently joined in acknowledging God's hand in the fact that they were safe and warm in the shelter of this home.

Julie went through her drawers for sweat suits for the ladies, and found others belonging to Mike for some of the men. When she walked into the kitchen, she noticed the young parents each holding a weary youngster.

"Let's get these children into sleeping bags. They look like they've had it for the day. Janice, I'll show you where your family can sleep. We have a houseful, so hopefully, you won't mind sharing one room with your husband's parents. You'll find extra blankets and pillows in the closet there." Julie started down the hall, followed by the young couple carrying the children.

The Hallmans and the older Mills continued their conversation at the table, as Linda refilled the coffee cups and set out sandwiches and cookies on the table. No one said a word about being hungry, but the food rapidly disappeared. Realizing the children had probably had nothing to eat, she filled a tray with a couple of sandwiches and two glasses of milk. When she knocked on the bedroom door, Janice said, "That's so thoughtful of you. The kids snacked on candy bars earlier, but really have had nothing since lunch. Thank you so much."

By 1:00 a.m., Julie had arranged sleeping places for her unexpected guests. Susan and Linda sat down to drink their first cup of coffee following dinner. Julie poured herself another cup and joined them at the table, relieved to sit down for a moment.

"Did you ever imagine your weekend would turn out like this, Julie?" laughed Susan. She had barely finished speaking when they heard pounding at the door.

"If that's someone else looking for shelter, we'll be hanging them from the ceiling," sighed Julie, wearily. She rose from the table and went to the door.

"We saw your light, and wondered if we might stay here for the night. My friend and I are stranded and don't know where we are. We're vacationing from New York and were warned to leave our automobile and climb to higher ground."

"Of course. Come in," said Julie to the two middle-aged women who had an air of superiority about them. "We have a rather full house, but if you don't mind taking whatever space is available, you're more than welcome."

"First of all, may we take a shower and get out of these wet clothes? If you could find us some robes and gowns, it would be wonderful," one of the women said. Her voice reminded Julie of a schoolteacher speaking to one of her pupils.

Susan and Linda looked at each other with an expression that conveyed more than words could say.

"I'm sorry, but because of the danger of running out of water, we can't allow you to shower," said Julie kindly.

"Not shower! But we're filthy from walking around in the rain and the mud," said the woman indignantly.

"We have seventeen people under our roof already, and we'll need safe drinking water before the storm is over. Our supply tank will not take care of showers. I'm sorry," said Julie, with a slight edge in her voice. "I'll get you some clean towels and washcloths so you will be able to clean up before you put on dry clothes."

"Just look at my beautiful white Dior slack suit," wailed the woman. "I don't know why I wanted to come out west anyway." Large diamonds flashed from both hands as she brushed mud and leaves to the floor from her clothing.

"I think if you get cleaned up and into bed, things will look better in the morning," said Julie in a conciliatory tone.

"We plan to get on a plane and fly out at the first possible opportunity," said the woman in exasperation.

Julie countered by replying, "You may not realize how lucky you are to be alive. You should count your blessings. Follow me, and I'll show you to the bathroom. There's another bed in the loft, but you will have to share with two other girls."

Julie could see the dismay on the woman's face, but she didn't say anything, fortunately for her. Julie's patience was nearly exhausted with the woman's haughty attitude.

Susan and Linda were snickering when Julie stepped back into the kitchen.

"Gals, let's go to bed before anything else happens. Do you realize it's two o'clock in the morning? I'm bushed, and I'm sure you are too. Our king size bed should accommodate three people for what's left of the night. If the guys come, they can pull out the hide a bed in the living room, but they may not come in until daylight. If I weren't so tired, I'd walk down to the river to check on them, but if we don't get to bed now, we may not get any sleep at all," said Julie.

She washed her cup in cold dishwater, rinsed it, and turned it upside down on the counter. "What else could happen tonight?"

Chapter 9

The Rescue

Sunday, August 1, 1976

The mist of the night before slowly dissipated, leaving a milky blanket of fog in the early morning hours. The seven people huddled on the mountain, aching with weariness and bone-chilling cold, began to stir. A pale yellow dawn began to creep over the mountains.

Jake pulled his tall frame to a standing position, stretched stiff limbs and rubbed his arms. He walked around the group to get his blood circulating. "Come on. Let's move to get warm. First of all, I think we should hunt for anything dry that might burn, and get a fire going. These cold, wet clothes aren't doing us any good."

Karyn stood up, feeling every aching bone in her body. The night seemed a hundred years long. Looking at the others who shared the bitter night, she was shocked to see how disheveled they looked in the dim morning light. It occurred to her she was a sight to behold herself. Running her fingers through her matted hair, she looked down at her mud-stained white slacks and muddy tennis shoes. She longed for a good hot shower and some warm, clean clothes. It would be awhile before the sun was up enough to dry their clothing. *Why would I worry about that? Will we find Jim this morning?*

Jake and Ron returned with a few pieces of dry wood from the inside of a rotten log. "I've got matches if someone has a little paper of some kind," said Jake.

Jill rummaged through her purse and found her grocery list and some store coupons.

Karyn pulled the wrapping paper from her plastic bag and handed it to Jake.

"This might get a fire started," said Jake, carefully arranging the paper, small trash, and the wood. He lit a cigarette and ignited the paper with a burning match. "It's going to take some coaxing to keep this fire going."

Each one stood eyeing the fire while it flickered tentatively, secretly praying it would become a blazing source of warmth.

Jake carefully tended the fire, until it began to catch on the larger pieces of wood. "Ron, you and Jack take the women back where we found the wood, and I'll keep an eye on the fire. Here's my knife. Try to dig some more dry wood out of the center of that log. And don't be too long! These chips are going to burn in a hurry."

Karyn was startled by a Stellars jay, scolding the intruders from high on his perch in a blue spruce.

Evidence of the storm lay all around. The ground was littered with leaves and branches. Columbine, Indian paintbrush, and yellow lupine were beaten to the earth by the force of the rain. The only beauty untouched was the evergreens. Tiny teardrops of moisture, collected on the pine needles, sparkled like diamonds when touched by the rays of the sun in the east.

All of them came back with something to feed the fire. As they crowded around, Debbie sidled up to Jill. "Mom, I'm hungry."

Karyn looked to see what remained of her candy and nuts. She passed them to Jill, who made sure everyone had some.

The sun crept higher over the mountain, and the day held the promise of warming up. When the warmth began to penetrate and clothing started to dry, the survivors felt more optimistic about their circumstances.

"Let's go back down the slope and see what happened during the night," said Jake. "There isn't much remaining of this fire, and it'll help us to move around." Jake had automatically assumed care for Karyn and the others, as well as his own family.

Picking their way through the tangle of rabbitbrush and cactus, they were half the morning retracing their steps down the mountain to where they could view the scene below. They were shocked by the devastation. Cars were mutilated pieces of junk in the muddy riverbed. The banks were eaten away by the force of the water. A road no longer existed where they had left their vehicles in the night. Nothing was familiar about the normally tranquil mountain stream. Huge boulders had washed down the canyon, pulverizing everything in their path. Trees were strewn across the river, along with the roof of someone's house. Debris of all kinds was caught in a tangled mass around the edge of the main channels. They stood numbed by the sight. Karyn began to sob. Jim didn't have a chance to survive unless he had come up the mountain. They hadn't seen or heard anyone else, which was strange.

Jill put her arm around Karyn's shoulder as they stood wordlessly surveying the destruction. The sound of a helicopter flying overhead broke the stunned silence. The chopper circled and flew west up the canyon.

Jake was the first to move. "Let's get on top of the hill and see what's going on. Maybe we've got some help up there." He started leading the group back up the mountain again.

They carefully picked their way up the hillside. It was sobering to think how narrowly they had escaped with their lives. As they made their way up the steep incline in the daylight, Jill said to Karyn, "I don't know how you ever found a path up here in the dark."

The sun was high overhead when they reached the top of the

rise once again. Jake picked up a leaflet dropped from the helicopter. "They've left us five army sleeping bags and a carton of army rations. There are instructions to signal if we need medical aid, or to let the pilot know everything is okay here. Yeah, for the army," Jake shouted, as he broke into the ration pack.

"Since we're going to be here for a while, I suggest we eat our rations and some of us climb into sleeping bags. We're all tired," said Jill. "It might be some time before we get out of here, and we don't want anyone sick."

Sheer exhaustion overcame Karyn as she snuggled into the comfort of a dry bag. She drifted off to sleep, still hearing Jake and Jill as they considered what efforts would be made for their rescue.

The noise of helicopters returning woke Karyn in the middle of a nightmare. She dreamed she was standing in the middle of the floodwaters and couldn't move. Someone kept calling to her for help, but she couldn't see anyone in the mist.

❖ ❖ ❖

Karyn had no idea how long she had been asleep when the noise of the chopper startled her.

Jill was shaking Ron, trying to rouse him. "Wake up. You can't possibly sleep through that noise."

The others gradually climbed out of their warm cocoons as a UH-1 Iroquois helicopter approached in the distance. The pilot circled a flat area to set down. Soon several National Guardsmen jumped out and started toward them.

"Is everyone okay here? We're going to take you to another location where we have a number of stranded survivors. Larger choppers will move you out in groups from there. If you will collect your belongings, we'll take off."

One of the guardsmen started to help Karyn with her sleeping bag. "Are you all right? You don't look like you feel too well."

"It's been a rough night. I'm missing a friend who drove up

the canyon with me. Have you picked up a young man named Jim, sandy hair, hazel eyes, and about six feet? He was going to move his car, and sent me up the mountain. I haven't seen him since."

"We're picking up survivors all along the canyon. Maybe he's in one of the other groups. I'll keep an eye out for him. Now let's get you on board."

Ron's eyes glowed with the excitement of a sixteen-year-old as he climbed into the chopper. "Wow! This is some machine."

Jill, Jake, and Debbie were helped into the chopper by another of the guardsmen. Mack and Sara followed. Sara eyed the machine tentatively and whispered to Mack, "What if I get sick? You know how I hate flying."

"Honey, it's going to be fine. Just don't look down and you'll be all right. You want to get home, don't you?"

When the guardsman handed Karyn up, Eric, in his Air Force flight uniform, grabbed her hand to pull her in. Their eyes locked in surprise. Startled beyond belief, he exclaimed, "Karyn, what are you doing here?"

Stunned to see him, she replied, "You're a long ways from California!"

"It's a long story. I'll tell you about it later." Releasing her hand, he stepped to the controls of the helicopter. Eric took off, circling over the treetops as they made their way to the emergency helipad. Karyn strained to see the river below, but could catch only a fleeting glimpse of the muddy flow, littered with the destruction from the night before.

As they hovered over the Merri Ax Café, a group of people were milling around. The survivors backed away so the chopper could land. Eric set the aircraft down in the parking lot where the Larimer County Command Post had been set up. The guardsmen provided containers with drinking water, hot coffee, sandwiches, and doughnuts. The food quickly disappeared, devoured by the hungry group who had, by now, missed several meals.

Once the evacuees were deposited on the ground, the chopper took off to pick up other survivors. Karyn wandered around in the assembly of people looking for Jim, and asking if anyone had seen him. Others in the cluster of anxious faces had missing family members, too. Karyn listened to a couple relate, "We were traveling up the road when we watched the car in front of us plunge off into the darkness and float down the river. We abandoned our car and climbed up the face of a rocky cliff in the pounding rain and darkness."

Some of the weary collection of survivors sat staring off into space, seemingly oblivious to everything around them. Others were compelled to talk about their narrow escape. A gray-haired woman sobbed, "I watched my husband being washed downstream, frantically trying to clutch a floating log, only to be carried away in the rushing current."

Each time the chopper came in, those with missing members of their party looked expectantly to see who would emerge from the aircraft. Some were rewarded, others saddened.

Eric looked at Karyn with sympathy while she stood waiting to see if Jim was among the passengers each time the chopper arrived. He addressed one of the guardsmen, "Why don't you get someone to start compiling names of the people here, and those who are missing. We can turn them over to the Red Cross." He handed them pads and pens.

One of the guardsmen said to Karyn, "We need to get the names of these people, and the names and phone numbers of the family members to be notified of their safety. We'll also need a list of the missing ones from this group. Do you think you could get someone to help you do that? Let's get the names of those coming in off the chopper on the next load as soon as we land."

Karyn explained the instructions to Jill and Jake.

"Sure we'll help. That beats sitting around here doing nothing," said Jill.

Jake tapped on the water container to get everyone's attention. "The Red Cross needs records of people at this location, and the names of those missing from your party. If you would line up in two lines, it would help us get the necessary information. Karyn, Jill and I will make a list of the people here if you get the names of those coming in on the chopper."

A smaller Kiowa brought in a party of three, and Karyn began taking names. The temporary distraction helped quell the anxiety she felt as each hour rolled by and there was no sign of Jim.

A young woman disembarking from the chopper cried, "I can't find my baby boy! Where is my baby?" Another couple slowly guided her from the aircraft. One of the guardsmen tried to comfort her with, "Ma'am, we'll do all we can to try to find him." There was a look of compassion on his face, but he shook his head in despair as he turned to walk back to the chopper.

Jake walked up to the guardsman standing by the helicopter. "When are you going to be able to get us out of this canyon? I don't like the looks of those clouds building up off to the west. These people can't stand another night out in this kind of weather."

"If the weather holds, the big Chinooks should get in to take you out this afternoon. We have people stranded all up and down the canyon. There is no way out except by air, or climbing over the mountain. Crews have tried to reconstruct a temporary road, but there's still too much water coming down Highway 34, and it keeps washing out. When the big Chinooks get here, this will go much faster. We're doing all we can."

Karyn shuddered as she thought about another night in the canyon. *How long will it be before all of us get home?* The very thought of another night renewed a chilling sense of dread. *What I wouldn't give for a nice hot shower and some clean clothes. How can I be concerned about that now?* The agony of not knowing what happened to Jim made everything else seem of little consequence by comparison.

It was two-thirty in the afternoon when an Iroquois chopper brought in seven more people. As the party disembarked from the last flight, Eric addressed the group. "This trip, we will evacuate anyone who needs medical attention. How many do we have?"

Jake spoke up. "The lady who lost her baby is in shock. We have another woman who might have a broken arm. Another is diabetic, and needs medication."

One of the guardsmen made his way through the crowd with an elderly gentleman who was suffering from hypothermia.

To the guardsmen, Eric said, "Let's get these people on board. We'll take the couple with two small children. That afternoon storm is moving in fast. We may not be able to make another flight."

Karyn stood by the helicopter completing her list of survivors as the guardsmen began assisting the medical evacuees. Suddenly, she felt as if the ground beneath her had begun to spin, making her nauseous.

Eric took one look at Karyn. " I think you'd better come in with us and turn those records into the Red Cross. They could probably use some help with contacting families and compiling lists of survivors. You look like you could use a little medical attention yourself."

Jake brought the rest of the completed lists and handed them to a guardsman.

"We're taking this young lady in, too," Eric said, nodding at Karyn. "Maybe she can locate her friend, as well as help us with these records."

Karyn didn't have the strength to protest.

It started to mist and the sky had become heavily overcast. The chance that helicopters would be able to make another flight grew slim. Karyn's heart ached for those people still stranded on the mountain.

Chapter 10

Tragic Aftermath

There was mass confusion at the rescue center located in Thompson Valley High School. Outside, sirens were screaming and the chop-chop of helicopters broke the silence. Inside, sniffling, sobbing, and subdued voices could be heard, along with the sound of telephones ringing and doors slamming in the background.

Volunteers were running from place to place trying to sort out the chaos as people continually streamed through the doors. An emergency phone system had been installed to take care of incoming and outgoing calls from desperate family members and friends. Members of the Red Cross and volunteers compiled names, trying to locate the whereabouts of out-of-state visitors, as well as local residents.

Karyn handed her list of survivors and those missing to a lady sitting at the records table.

"Thank you so much. This will be a big help to us. Honey, you don't look very well. You had better see one of the doctors over there."

When Karyn looked at the line waiting to see a doctor, she decided to bypass that. Choking back the emotion that threatened to overwhelm her, she sat down on a red gym mat provided for survivors, trying to decide what to do next. She had survived a night of terror, only to realize the ordeal wasn't over yet. She had to find out about Jim.

Ladies were serving cups of hot soup and sandwiches at a table across the gym. *Something hot would make me feel much better.* Walking to the serving table, she picked up a cup of soup and a sandwich and sat down on one of the gym mats. Sipping the hot soup, she realized how weak and hungry she was from the terrifying experience of the previous night.

Looking up she saw Eric making his way through the crowd to where she sat.

"Are you all right? You didn't look too good when we brought you in."

"I'm feeling much better now that I'm a little warmer and have had something to eat."

"Have you heard anything about your friend?"

"I need to check at the records desk to see if they have any information about him."

"I've been asking the other pilots, but they haven't picked up anyone with that general description."

"There is no way I can go home until I know what happened to him." Tears squeezed from her eyes and she dried them with the back of her hand.

"I'll keep trying to see what I can find out, but it looks like we're grounded until the weather clears a little."

"There isn't enough help at the records desk. I think I'll go over and see if I can lend them a hand. If you hear anything about Jim, I'll be there."

Eric helped Karyn up from the mat. They threaded their way through the crowd to the records table.

When Eric turned to walk away, Karyn said, "Thanks for your help. Let me know if you hear anything. By the way, you didn't tell me why you happened to be on this rescue mission."

"My friends and I had planned to do some whitewater rafting on the Colorado. I flew in yesterday morning, and we heard the news on TV last night. I figured they would need pilots for an emergency rescue mission, so I volunteered."

"You can't imagine how surprised I was to see you here."

"No more surprised than I was when I helped you into the chopper."

"Thanks again, Eric. Let me know if you hear anything."

"Sure will, Karyn."

A gray-haired lady, standing beside the table, broke out with heart-wrenching sobs. Karyn put her arm around the woman's shoulder in a comforting gesture. "Is there something I can do to help you?" she asked.

"My husband is gone, and there is nothing anyone can do to help me," she wailed. "The rescuers tried to reach him, but the current was too swift."

Karyn listened intently as the woman sobbed while relating her story.

❖ ❖ ❖

Eric paused in the sea of people to look back over his shoulder at Karyn. The surprise of seeing her in these circumstances jarred him to the core. He watched her with more than a casual interest. The ease with which she expressed compassion to the obvious stranger touched a sensitive response in Eric. She seemed so vulnerable. *Is that why I'm feeling so protective? After all, she has some kind of relationship with Jim or she wouldn't be taking this so hard.* Despite the thought, he continued to stare at her from a distance. The dark circles around her eyes accentuated the pallor of her skin. With hair stringing around her face, and her white slacks soiled with mud, she was not exactly a raving beauty at this moment. The inner strength she exhibited surprised him, considering what she had been through. He moved to the door to join the men at the helipad, and Karyn approached the records table.

A lady in a Red Cross uniform, who seemed to be in charge, was giving instruction to several volunteers. "You may put that stack of blankets over by the red gym mats."

"Could you use a helping hand?" asked Karyn. "I would be glad to do whatever I can."

"We certainly could. I'm Jenny Stover. If you could help us with compiling names, addresses and family members of survivors and victims, it would help tremendously. A local company will be providing us with computers to enter the information, but until they get them set up, we'll have to do it manually. Can you type?"

"Yes. By the way, I'm Karyn Anderson. Show me where to begin."

"Before you get started, we need to find you a change of clothes and give you a chance to clean up. There are showers in the restrooms with fresh towels and toilet supplies. I'll find something for you to put on. Then we'll get you set up right here."

As Jenny left, Karyn looked around the gym. The suffering she saw made her heart ache. The desolation etched on the faces of survivors caused her throat to constrict. People came wrapped in blankets, their clothing torn off their bodies while they had struggled to escape the raging waters. Sobbing family members, overcome with grief and shock at their personal loses, wandered aimlessly. A little girl clutched her tattered, muddy doll and refused to let go of it when a nurse tried to help her. The doll's appearance was a mirror image of the child herself. Karyn turned away, dabbing at the tears welling up in her eyes as she witnessed the child's distress when she was asked to relinquish her only tangible possession.

Jenny touched Karyn's arm, startling Karyn. "I hope this will fit you. People in the community have responded so quickly that we do have some clothing to offer survivors coming in."

"Clean and dry will feel wonderful," said Karyn, heading for the showers.

Standing in the shower, Karyn felt the luxury of the warm water flowing over her aching body. The warmth began to make her feel drowsy and like a lead weight. Lathering the soap generously on the washcloth, the delicate fragrance of the soap reminded her of how often she had taken the simple act of showering for granted. Rinsing with cool water, she climbed out and vigorously dried with a towel. Jenny had found her a seersucker jumpsuit which Karyn pulled over her underthings. Brushing her dark, wavy hair, she pulled the sides back into her barrette.

"You look much better," Jenny said as Karyn came back to the table. "We'll put you right here. I'll get someone on the speaker to let survivors know we need to get this information as soon as possible. By now most of them have had something to eat, and an opportunity to collect their thoughts. We'll be dealing with a lot of pain. Can you handle that?"

"I understand the emotions they are feeling. I have a friend who is lost, and I have no idea where he is. I'm here until I find out what happened to him."

"I'm so sorry," said Jenny. She looked intently at Karyn. "Are you sure you want to do this?"

"Yes," replied Karyn. "It will help to have something to do while I wait, and there is so much misery here."

"Please, may I have your attention." A voice from the loud speaker helped the confused group of people to focus on someone who could tell them what must be done.

"This is Ray Black from the Red Cross. We know all of you have been through a difficult ordeal. You're weary and worried about family and friends. In order for us to help you locate those missing, we must ask you to help us by supplying all the information that you can concerning the location of possible victims. We must also have information concerning the families here in the rescue center that we can relay to family and friends.

"Phone lines are jammed now, with people trying to contact someone who can give them this information. We need to compile this data to have it available for emergency services, and for those trying to locate family and friends.

"There is a records table located at the west entrance of the building. Will you please see the volunteers working there? Most importantly, please do not leave the building until you have provided this information to the volunteers. Thank you."

Grief and shock was registered on the faces of people as they came through the lines to relay pertinent information. Many sobbed as they related the tragedies of family and friends. It was difficult for them to be brief, and was equally impossible for the women recording the necessary details to keep the lines moving without seeming unsympathetic to the grief of the survivors.

After several hours, Jenny came to Karyn. "You'd better take a break. There's coffee and doughnuts at a table near the door. How is it going so far?"

"It's so hard to listen to the stories and to keep recording the information as well. These poor families."

"There are some local ministers coming in who will be able to deal with grief trauma. They'll be a tremendous help to us. I'll send someone over to cover for you," said Jenny, hurrying off to assist another volunteer.

Karyn typed until her fingers were numb. Glad to stand up and take a break, she was surprised when she looked at her watch and realized she had lost track of time. It was 5:10 p.m. As she sipped hot coffee, she looked out the window to see the sun shinning through the clouds. Buses resumed bringing in other survivors from the helipad. *I had better get back to my table. I just hope they're able to get everyone in from the canyon before dark.*

When Karyn walked back to the receiving area, men were unloading computers. "We'll have this set up for you in a few minutes. This will make your work go a whole lot faster," said a man dressed in a business suit with a name tag reading Business Tec, Inc.

A young, auburn-haired woman who had taken Karyn's place, smiled and said, "I'm Cathy Preston, another volunteer. You must be Karyn. When they get the computers set up, we will be working here together."

The crushing stream of survivors coming through the lines gave them little time for conversation. People kept pouring in the doors. Doctors and nurses quickly administered first aid to the injured. The emergency cases were whisked away in ambulances to the hospital.

Huge Chinook helicopters landed with survivors from groups who had been transported earlier to assembly areas by the smaller aircraft. It became extremely important to get stranded people off the mountain before they were forced to spend a second night there.

Three reporters came through the door with their cameras. Two uniformed policemen quickly moved to the door to turn them away. There was a protest from one of the more aggressive male reporters at being denied entrance.

"These families have been through a terrible ordeal. The last thing they need is cameras going off in their faces. There will be plenty of time for their stories later," said the officer in charge as he backed the group out the door. "The Red Cross will be glad to make a statement to the press at a later time."

Refrigerated trucks provided a temporary morgue for the bodies that began to arrive. Family names were called out on the loud speaker. The tension mounted ten fold. Some of the bodies could be identified by wallets or personal affects that still remained in their clothing. For those families, the questions were over, but the real grief had just begun. Emotions ran deep in the room—sadness, anger, grief, and love. Ministers came to their aid in an effort to support them through the worst of the trauma and help them begin resuming their lives. For some, it meant transportation to their homes locally, or out of state. Others, whose homes or businesses were destroyed, had to begin the process of determining their remaining assets.

❖ ❖ ❖

Dusk closed in as pilots made their last trip out of the canyon. It had been a trying day for them. Flying between narrow canyon walls, with low ceilings and wind currents, made flying hazardous to pilots and aircraft. They faced not only the tension of difficult flying conditions, but also the pressure of getting stranded people back to some shelter. The stress took its toll on them, as well as the survivors they brought out.

Eric shrugged his shoulders and twisted his head to relieve the tension in his neck and back. He was tired. It seemed unreal to think he had left California yesterday morning, followed by eighteen holes of golf and a night rescue mission. For a fleeting second, Eric thought about the rafting trip he had planned with friends. *How can I think about rafting at a time like this? There are still survivors to be rescued, and the number of victims is still mounting. I can't believe I'm even on this mission!*

He had met some resistance when he volunteered at Lowry Air Force base.

"We'll have to get clearance from your commanding officer at Beale," said the officer in charge. "We're in a bind for pilots because of the extreme urgency of the rescue mission. We can always use support personnel. I'll see what I can do."

Cleared for support personnel, Eric joined the crew of volunteers who were immediately flown to the relief site in Loveland. They assisted the Sheriff's Department in getting the helipad set up between Loveland and the base of the canyon. Several small helicopters, supplied by a local agricultural firm, were the first on the scene to aid in the rescue. One of the National Guard pilots had to be relieved because of illness. Eric was assigned to fly his Iroquois.

Throughout the day he had continued to pick up stranded people to transfer them to an area where they could be flown out by the large Chinooks. When the larger aircraft arrived, the weather was no longer cooperative. Later in the day, the sun popped through the cloud cover, and the pilots were able to get the machines in the air. Evacuation resumed in earnest.

When Eric set the aircraft down with each load, he asked about Jim. So far, no one by that name and description had been brought in. He couldn't help but wonder how serious the relationship was between Jim and Karyn. *Why of all people does she keep coming to my mind?*

He dated several young women, but none of them seriously. His first love was flying, and all else just fit into that picture in a secondary way. He had been content to leave it that way. *Why does her image keep popping into my mind at unexpected times?*

Eric's thoughts turned to flying. For as long as he could remember, he wanted to fly. It probably had to do with the fact that his father was a pilot in World War II. His mother had proudly shown him the pictures of his father in uniform, standing beside his plane. After the war, his father returned home to fly for a commercial airline on the West coast. Eric continued to put model airplanes together as a youngster, carefully crafting every detail, while dreaming of flying himself.

Dusk closed in as the helicopter neared the helipad. Eric breathed a sigh of relief. The flight crews had done all they could for one day. It was hard to think about leaving anyone still stranded through the night. He set the chopper down with its load of human cargo, beset by nature's angry turn of events. While the crew helped unload the survivors, Eric walked to the construction trailer that served as a temporary operations office. There, the crew had gathered to get last minute instructions from Larimer County's Operation Officer in charge of the rescue operations. He and Sheriff Wilson had coordinated all the various plans for the following day.

"Tomorrow we hope to be able to bring out all of the people we've located in the upper canyon," said the Sheriff. "From weather reports we have received, fog is forecast for the early morning hours, but it should clear out by mid-morning.

"Highway crews hope to be able to construct a temporary road along Highway 34. Their efforts have been futile today because of the amount of water still coming down the channels. Ground crews will be responsible for people stranded in the lower part of the canyon.

"You men have done a tremendous job today. We would all liked to have had better flying weather, but there was nothing we could do about that. We were able to drop sleeping bags and some supplies to people still left in groups on the hillsides. We want you here at 0600 in the morning to get these machines ready to get in the air as soon as the weather permits.

"A truck is available to transport you to the National Guard Armory in Fort Collins for a hot meal and a good night's sleep. The truck will be leaving in thirty minutes. Thanks again for a job well done. You are dismissed."

Chapter 11

Sorting Out the Chaos

K aryn and Cathy left their computer stations only once during the afternoon. Staff members from the Red Cross came by with coffee to serve the volunteers who were too busy to leave their stations.

Some of the congestion began to clear out as the rescue operations added personnel to help the victims. Agencies were set up to assist with various needs to help families resume their lives. Loveland motels, as well as private individuals, opened their doors to stranded visitors until the details of transportation could be worked out. Wives of volunteer firemen brought blankets, pillows, coffee and hot chocolate mixes. Volunteers transported local people to their homes, and vacationers to homes housing stranded visitors. Many people spent the second night on mats in the school, refusing to leave until they had some word concerning lost family members.

Survivors consoled each other as they shared the horrors they had experience in the night. "I can't believe I'm still alive," said a young woman. "Our house was washed down the river like matchsticks. The road in front of our house disintegrated before our eyes, leaving us nowhere to flee but up the mountain. My husband is still looking for his family."

Other families, torn asunder by the raging torrent, wept as the temporary shock wore off, and they were faced with the grim reality of death and destruction.

Jenny came up to stand behind Karyn. "I'm sending you two home before you drop. Someone will relieve you here in a few minutes."

"I can't go home tonight," said Karyn. "There is still no word about Jim. I need to stay, at least until they bring in those stranded on the mountain. I'll call a friend in town and see if she can put Cathy and me up for the night."

"You two look absolutely beat. I could use your help again tomorrow, if that isn't too much to ask. Will you be able to do that?" asked Jenny.

Both nodded their heads in reply. "I need to talk to my boss," said Karyn. "He probably has no idea what happened to me, and he'll be expecting me tomorrow morning for work. With telephones so busy, I haven't had a chance to call him."

"I'll free up a line immediately so you can call," said Jenny, starting toward the room she was using for an office.

Karyn followed and waited.

"You'll be able to call out now. Karyn, I've been watching you all day. You're so good with people. There is a gentleness about you that people love, and children respond to. I want you to know how much that means to these families." Jenny gave Karyn a warm hug before she left the office.

Karyn dialed Wade's home number, and the phone rang five times before Helen picked it up.

"Helen, is Wade there? This is Karyn."

"Karyn! We've been trying all day to get some information about you. After listening to the news, I tried to call the rescue center, but the lines were always busy. When I tried to phone your friends up the canyon, all I got was a recording saying the phone lines were out. We have been so worried. Where are you?"

"I'm at the rescue headquarters in Loveland. I'm fine, but they haven't been able to locate Jim. We got separated when the flooding started, and I don't know where he is." Karyn's voice broke at that point.

"Karyn, do you want me to come after you? You've been through a terrible ordeal."

"No. Just tell Wade that I'm not sure when I'll be in the office. I don't want to leave Loveland until I get some word about Jim. I need to talk to his parents in Chicago."

"Don't worry about things in the office. I can go in and do what needs to be done until you get back. We're so relieved that you're okay. Let us know when you hear something about Jim."

Karyn hung up the receiver, suddenly overcome with numbing weariness. Her shoulders sagged, and her eyes were tired and bloodshot from the lack of sleep. *How can I get through another emotionally exhausting day like this? I must get some sleep. I have to call Cindy to see if she has room for Cathy and me tonight.*

"Cindy."

"Karyn, what in the world are you up to this time of night?" exclaimed Cindy.

"It's a long story. Right now, I'm wondering if you could put up two very weary girls who are looking for a bed for the night?"

"Of course. I would love to have you. Karyn, are you all right? What's going on? Where are you?" demanded Cindy.

"We're at the flood relief station at Thompson High School. Could you pick us up? We don't have a car."

"I'll be there in fifteen minutes. Meet me at the front entrance. I've been listening to the news all day and can't believe what happened!"

When Cindy saw the exhaustion in Karyn's face, she knew her friend had been through a harrowing experience. Shocked at

Karyn's general appearance, Cindy was quick to respond. "Karyn, you look awful. You look like you could use a good night's sleep."

Karyn made brief introductions as she wearily slid into the front seat of Cindy's car. Her eyes felt dry and gritty from lack of sleep.

When the three women walked into Cindy's two-bedroom apartment, Cindy lost no time in trying to make her two overnight guest as comfortable as possible.

"What you need is something to eat and a good hot shower. Then you can tell me all about what happened. There are fresh towels in the bathroom, and I'll lay out some gowns and robes on the beds in the guest room."

Cindy flipped on the TV while Karyn and Cathy took turns showering. She sucked in her breath at the enormity of the latest update of the canyon tragedy.

"The entire 2,700 square miles of Larimer County have been declared a disaster area. The Big Thompson River is believed to have crested at thirty feet in its passage through the narrows.

"In Loveland," continued the newscaster, "rescue efforts included the establishment of a Medivac heliport to accommodate more than a dozen evacuation helicopters provided through Lowry Air Force Base and the Colorado National Guard from Buckley Field in Denver. Rescue workers are still trying to determine the number of dead and missing as they search the canyon. It is estimated that there are more than one hundred dead as a result of this weekend tragedy."

While Cindy listened to the grim report, she started frying bacon and scrambling eggs for her two houseguests.

Channel 7 continued reporting. "A spokesman for the U.S. Weather Service in Denver said the flooding resulted from extremely moist air masses and abnormally slow wind currents.

"The storm that dumped massive amounts of water on Estes Park was virtually stationary, whereas most storms travel around twenty miles per hour. That stationary front was responsible for creating havoc in the canyon below.

"The State Patrol sent three officers into the canyon with loud speakers telling people to get out, but many people did not heed the warnings. Deputies who drove through the canyon said they warned some people as many as three times, but many stayed anyway—a mistake some paid for with their lives.

"We'll keep you posted on the latest events as news continues to come into Channel 7."

When Karyn came into the kitchen, Cindy flipped off the TV and popped some bread into the toaster. While they ate their meal at the kitchen table, Karyn related what had happened. "It's begun to seem like days ago Jim and I drove up the canyon." The intense drama of the last twenty-four hour's experiences had evoked all Karyn's emotions just to be able to cope with events that surrounded her. All the adrenaline-related energy began to dissipate. *Will my life ever be the same again?*

Cathy sat in silence for some time, trying to create a visual image as Karyn recapped what happened the night of the flood. Then she sighed. "Witnessing the trauma for the survivors at the rescue center was one thing, but to imagine the chaos in the mountains is quite another!"

"Here I am keeping both of you up after such an exhausting day. Much as I would like to sit here and talk all night, you two need to get to bed. We'll finish this conversation in the morning. Okay?"

Gratefully, Karyn gave her friend a hug and responded, "It can't be too soon for me!"

Cathy thanked Cindy for her hospitality, and the two promptly headed for bed.

During the night, Karyn awoke with a sudden start. She had been dreaming and reliving the events of the torturous climb up the hill in the dark. It took her a few moments to realize where she was. She was perspiring and her body ached with weariness. Glancing around the room to make sure she was really safe, she turned over and fell into a deep sleep.

Awakened by the aroma of fresh coffee floating into the bedroom and the sound of Cathy and Cindy talking, Karyn stretched and climbed out of bed. She felt rested and enormously hungry. Slipping on a robe and walking into the kitchen, she found Cindy and Cathy seated at the bar having coffee, juice and fresh pecan rolls.

"We thought you were going to sleep forever," teased Cindy. "I didn't want to disturb you, so we decided to eat without you."

"That's fine. I really intended to be up and back to the school by this time. Maybe they can tell me something this morning," Karyn remarked, taking her place at the breakfast bar.

"I threw your clothes in the washer and dryer, but they are hardly in any shape to wear. Why don't you check my closet. If there's anything in there you can wear, help yourself. And, Karyn, your mom called after you went to bed last night."

"She did?" Karyn set her coffee cup down and asked, "Did she say what she wanted?"

"She'd been trying to get you all day yesterday. When she heard the news on TV, she wanted to know what was going on. Of course, she had no idea you were on the scene at the time. The operator kept telling her all the circuits were busy. It was a miracle she got through when she did."

"What did you tell her?"

"I gave her the barest of details so as not to alarm her, but she wants you to call as soon as you can."

Karyn could imagine her mother getting more nervous as the day progressed when she couldn't reach Karyn. They usually called each other over the weekend, but because of the plans Karyn and Jim had made, she had not called home.

Her parents had always had a close relationship with their two daughters, Karyn and Corrine, even though both women were pursuing their own lives in distant states. Corrine had married a dentist and lived in Oregon. Karyn had moved to Colorado to pursue her master's degree and ski the Colorado slopes.

When Karyn tried to call her mother, all available lines were still busy. "I'll have to wait until later to call home. We need to get back to help at the relief station. I have to see if they have any word about Jim."

The weather had cleared, and the noise of choppers could be heard in the distance.

Cindy let the women out of the car in front of the school and said, "I'll plan on both of you staying with me this evening. After work, I'll drop by to see how things are going."

It was Monday morning, and Loveland buzzed with activity as a result of the flood. Ambulances screamed on route to area hospitals. Traffic policemen were trying to keep the flow of vehicles around the rescue center moving in an orderly fashion, making it possible for medical units and rescue personnel to get where they were needed.

When Karyn and Cathy walked into the rescue center, they could readily see how monumental the task had become. Red Cross volunteers were seated at the additional computers, which helped to relieve the long lines. By now other relief agencies had arrived to help staff services needed for food, transportation, funds for travel, and caring for the injured until they could be transported to area hospitals. The various agencies occupied different areas of the school to relieve the congestion in the gym.

The Salvation Army had rapidly responded to the emergency call, and was among the first of the agencies at the scene. They had set up their canteen outside the school to provide food for the law enforcement personnel, and those involved in the rescue operations.

Food, clothing, and blankets were being carried in by volunteers, providing essential items to people coming in with nothing left but what they were wearing.

Karyn started to her workstation through the milling crowd

when someone touched her arm. Turning, she was surprised to see Jill and Jake smiling warmly.

"Am I glad to see you! When did the pilots bring you in? I kept looking for you yesterday afternoon. Is everyone okay?" asked Karyn, the questions tumbling from her mouth in one breath.

"We seem to be none the less for wear considering our two nights camping out," laughed Jake in his hearty, robust manner.

"Why are you still here at the rescue center?" asked Jill in surprise. Then a knowing look crossed her face. "You still haven't heard anything about Jim?"

"So far, nothing. The fact that he hasn't been located doesn't look good at this point," sighed Karyn, as her eyes misted and her voice trembled.

"Oh, Karyn. I'm so sorry to hear that," said Jill, looking into Karyn's tortured face.

"I don't know what to tell his parents." Her lip quivered, and she looked away to avoid their eyes. "Mom said his folks were frantic with worry when they tried to contact him and couldn't get through. I must let them know something tonight. They need to know that rescue crews are doing everything possible to locate the missing."

"Maybe they'll find Jim today. Those fly boys have done a good job considering how unsettled the weather has been. I'm amazed they could bring us out when they did," said Jake, as he moved his hand across the two-day stubble on his face.

"So what are your plans now?" asked Karyn.

"First, we're going to get cleaned up. They tell me we can shower here, and maybe find something decent to wear. Then we'll proceed to plan B," said Jake. He shifted his restless feet as he contemplated the next move. "We may have to take the long way back to Estes or put up in a motel, if there's anything available."

"Whatever we do," said Jill, with a yawn she made no effort to conceal, "I'm ready for a soft bed and eight hours of sleep.

Debbie is already asleep on a gym mat in the corner."

"Let's check with Jenny and see if there might be a motel available in the area. It's a problem trying to accommodate so many people."

Jenny was checking computer records when Karyn approached her.

"Do we have any motels available for a family of four from Estes? They have spent two nights on the mountain and look exhausted."

"If they don't mind going to Fort Collins, we have a shuttle leaving within the hour for CSU's dorms. The chairman of housing has made Braiden Hall available for families needing temporary shelter. They are also providing free meals on campus."

"At this point, we will take anything just to be able to get some rest," said Jill with a weary sigh when Karyn relayed the information.

"Oh, Honey, why don't we try to get home?" asked Jake. "We can rent a car and take the Lyons road to Estes."

"Then you'll just have to come back after us because Debbie and I are going to bed!" said Jill, her jawline set with determination.

"Maybe you're right," Jake acquiesced as he glanced at his wife with concern.

Karyn felt like a bystander while she witnessed this family discussion taking place. She needed to get back to her computer.

"It's so good to see both of you again. I can't tell you how much it meant to me to bump into you two in the dark of night. What a terrifying night! Let me give each of you a hug, and then I must get back to work."

"I have to say that you looked pretty lost and lonely when you stumbled into our group," said Jake. He wrapped his big arms around Karyn and shook his head for emphasis.

Turning to leave, Jill said, "Be sure and look us up when you're in Estes. We're in the phone book."

It was one o'clock when Jenny came to say, "Don't you think it's about time for you two to break for lunch? It would be best if you could take turns leaving your machines. I'll see if I can find someone to relieve you."

Karyn heard someone call to her as she moved through the crowd on her way to the cafeteria. She turned to see Eric weaving his way through the crowd toward her.

"Is there any information about Jim?" asked Eric. "I've been checking the list of people brought in and still nothing."

Karyn shook her head in response. "His name hasn't shown up in our records either. How complete is the evacuation up to this point?"

Eric's brow furrowed. "We should be able to bring out all the survivors we've located up on top today, but the teams going through the lower canyon will take longer. It looks like they are getting a temporary road through there now."

"I was just going to get something to eat. Have you had any lunch?"

"No, and I'm starved. I'm off duty for an hour, so let's see what they have."

Karyn and Eric picked up a tray and moved through the lunch line. There were two kinds of soup and a variety of sandwiches to choose from. They made their way to a partially empty table.

"This has been a hard day for the people we've been bringing in," said Eric. "Last night they had hope some of their loved ones would show up. Today the chance of that seems much slimmer. Do you feel the same way about Jim?"

"During the time we spent on the mountain, I was just sure he would come up the hill or wander through the timber. As people have related how narrowly they escaped the floodwater, I began to feel there was less chance of him getting out alive. I just have to know."

"I don't mean to be nosy, but was he someone special in your life?" asked Eric with an attentive look.

"It was nothing serious, but we had fun together. Jim and I met in a speech class at CSU. We discovered we were both from the Chicago area and struck up a friendship."

"I really haven't had a chance to ask you what happened. Do you feel like talking about it?"

"We were on our way up the canyon to visit friends for the weekend when it started flooding. A patrolman warned us to abandon our cars and climb to higher ground because of the water coming down the river. Jim had a new silver Porsche and decided to try to move it closer to the canyon wall. That's the last time I saw him." Karyn's mouth trembled and her voice broke.

"He insisted I start climbing and follow some other people getting out of their cars."

As she skimmed over the story, Eric sensed the depth of pain beneath it. He wanted to console her, but all he could think to say was, "I'm sorry," as he looked into her troubled face.

Karyn took a deep breath and struggled to maintain her composure. Eric was silent a moment while Karyn dried her eyes with a tissue.

"I'm sorry we haven't been able to locate him. How much longer do you plan to stay here?"

"I need to get home tonight. When I called my boss he said to take as much time as I needed. There doesn't seem to be much reason to stay here if they don't find Jim today. What about you?"

"I have to report back for duty in California on Thursday. I'd like to see you again before I leave. Do you think you would feel up to dinner tomorrow evening? Some place that doesn't look like a cafeteria in the middle of a crisis?"

The irony of the statement caused Karyn to smile, erasing the worried expression etched on her face and the sadness from her eyes.

"Yes, I'd like that. If there is no news of Jim by tonight, I have to get back to my job. Tomorrow I'll be back in Fort Collins."

"What's your address there?"

Karyn scratched the information and her phone number on one of the napkins.

Eric tucked the napkin in his uniform pocket. "I'll pick you up about seven. One of the guys told me the Charco Broiler has some great steaks. Does that sound all right to you?"

"Steak sounds wonderful. I hate to run off, but I need to get back to the computer to relieve Cathy. Thanks for the listening ear. I'll see you tomorrow night."

Both walked off to resume their separate duties, and Karyn thought, *What a strange situation in which to meet Eric again. What a caring, charming man.*

There was something so unreal about everything that was happening to her. *Why had she just agreed to meet someone she barely knew for dinner the following night? What on earth had she been thinking?*

Eric, not normally given to impulsive behavior, smiled to himself as he walked out to the helipad.

Chapter 12

A Dinner Date

Tears came to Karyn's eyes as she watched a family reunited after two days of wondering what happened to the other family members. The grandparents had gone to Denver for the weekend, leaving their daughter, son-in-law and grandchildren in their cabin near Cedar Cove for a vacation. Water surrounded their cabin at the same time they heard the bullhorn across the river. Pure panic seized them when water began pouring into the first floor. Rushing to the second floor, they were able to crawl out a back window, drop to the roof of a deck and escape up the mountain. Later, they watched as the cabin was swept into the raging channel.

Seven telephones continued to ring in the distance as operators relayed information concerning the safety of family and friends. Early reports estimated nearly 800 missing. That number was reduced to 225 as the rescue operations continued. It was a joy to be able to pass on information concerning those who had been rescued. Special operators were chosen to break the sad news of tragic deaths and convey their sympathy to families who had not been so fortunate.

It was after five o'clock when Cindy came by to see if Karyn had any news about Jim. "Still no news?"

"Nothing, Cindy. I was so sure they would find him today." Karyn's lower lip trembled and her eyes misted.

"You need to get out of here. When would you like me to pick you up this evening? I'll go home now and fix something for dinner. Do you think you can get out of here by seven?"

"Yes, she can," said Jenny. She came up behind Karyn in time to answer Cindy's question. "She's been here long enough! We'll find someone to relieve her."

"Jenny, I need to get back to my job tomorrow. I hate to leave while there is still so much to be done, but if Jim was still alive, they surely would have found him by now. I plan to go home tonight. I don't think I can struggle through another day."

"I understand how difficult it must be for you. I think that's a wise decision. The rescue personnel say most of the people are in from the hillsides. It will be another day before they will be able to make sure everyone in the lower canyon is accounted for. Weeks may go by before all the bodies can be recovered. This is going to take much longer than anyone anticipated. Thank you for all your help for the past two days. It was wonderful to have volunteers like you and Cathy."

Two hours passed rapidly. Karyn heard Cindy's voice over the noises that surrounded her. Are you two ready to go?" asked Cindy, approaching the table where Karyn and Cathy were entering data.

"Just as soon as I finish this entry. How is it coming with you, Cathy?"

"I'll be finished here as soon as I turn these lists into Jenny. Cindy, will it be a problem for you to drop me off here by nine thirty? My brother Mark will be here to pick me up."

"Need you ask? Come on. I'll be taking Karyn to Fort Collins after dinner."

When the women turned to leave, Karyn overheard someone say, "They brought in more bodies from the lower canyon this afternoon." Karyn paused to look at the man speaking.

"Karyn, come right now! You've had a grueling day, and there is nothing you can do tonight," said Cindy. Her tone was motherly and scolding. "Let it rest."

Knowing she was right, Karyn turned and together they walked out the door. "I don't think I could deal with a shock like that tonight."

When Cathy and Karyn walked into Cindy's kitchen, they were surprised to see the table set with candles and flowers. Soft dinner music floated from the stereo in the livingroom.

"What's the occasion for the dinner party?" Karyn asked.

"You both need some cheering up after the last few days. Just a little way of saying you two are terrific. Now get ready for dinner. I'm putting it on in two minutes."

Long after the lemon chicken with rice, asparagus, tossed salad, and chocolate cheesecake was gone, the women were still sitting at the dinner table discussing the events of the past three days. Turning to Cathy, Cindy asked, "How did you get involved in volunteering at the rescue center?"

"Mark and I had started up the canyon to visit his girlfriend's family in Estes for the weekend, and we were turned back at the mouth of the canyon. We heard the horrible news on the radio. He's a med student doing his internship, and we just stopped at the rescue center to see if we could help. It was utter chaos during those first few hours. He had to get back to school, or he'd still be there."

Cathy rose to say, "This has been wonderful, Cindy, but I must go. Thank you for generous hospitality on such short notice, and under such difficult circumstances."

"I must go, too. As soon as I can get through, I need to call my folks. Our friends up the canyon still don't know what happened to us."

They left Cathy at the school entrance and Karyn gave her a hug. "We'll have to get together under happier circumstances. It's been nice to work with you, Cathy."

"Bye, Cindy, and thanks for everything," said Cathy, as she turned to walk into the building.

✤ ✤ ✤

Karyn turned to get out of Cindy's car in front of her condo and stared at the unlighted windows. "Home never looked so good to me as it does right now. I'd invite you in, but I'd be poor company at this hour."

"Forget it. So what do you plan to do about notifying Jim's parents?" asked Cindy. An expression of sympathy crossed her face. "I don't envy you that job."

"I must tell them he is still missing, and we haven't any more information at this point. It will be so difficult for them. They had another son killed by a drunken driver several years ago. Cindy, thanks for everything. You've been wonderful, and I can't tell you how much it has meant to have a friend like you. I'll call you tomorrow."

"Are you going back to work tomorrow?"

"Yes. I told Wade I couldn't just sit around waiting for some news," sighed Karyn. She closed the car door and slowly walked up the steps.

The telephone was ringing when Karyn walked into the condo. She picked up the phone to hear her mother say, "Karyn, we have been worried sick about you. Tell us what happened."

"Jim and I were going up the canyon to have dinner with friends. We were caught in a terrible rainstorm, which started the flooding. He wouldn't leave his car." Once more the dreaded tears came and her voice broke. "He...told me to go...and he would follow me...but he wanted to move his car first...and he never came!"

"Oh, Honey. I'm so sorry. Have you talked to Jim's parents?"

"No. I just came home from the rescue center. Oh, Mom, they can't find Jim!" No longer able to camouflage the pain, Karyn burst out crying.

"Sweetheart, what do you want us to do?" Mrs. Anderson paused to give Karyn a chance to regain her voice. "Would it help if your Dad and I went to see Jim's parents? They've been calling us to see if we had heard from you."

"Mom, would you please?" Karyn blew her nose and wiped the tears from her eyes. "I'm not sure I can talk to them right now...Tell them...Jim is still missing. I stayed...hoping rescue crews would find him. Oh, Mom,...they started bringing in bodies..." Karyn's voice cracked with emotion.

"Honey, we're terribly sorry about Jim. We'll be praying they find him."

"Oh, Mom. It's just awful." Karyn sobbed. "I just can't talk about it anymore tonight."

"I can imagine how difficult it must be for you. I'll say good night, and we'll talk to you in the morning. Go to bed and get a good night's rest, Sweetheart."

Karyn sighed with relief as she hung up the phone. How she dreaded making that call. There were no words for the enormity of events that had taken place in the last three days. She had continued to hope there might be some good news, but today she felt it was no longer possible. What would Jim's parents think when they heard Karyn was alive and knew nothing about what happened to Jim? *Did I do the right thing when I left him there? Why was he so insistent on moving his car?*

Even though it was ten-thirty, she knew she should call Wade to say she would be in for work in the morning. She dried the tears, blew her nose, and went to the kitchen for a drink of water before she picked up the phone to dial.

Karyn's voice sounded hoarse over the line when Wade answered. "Are you sure you feel up to that so soon?"

"I can't stand another day of sitting around waiting for some news. As soon as the rescue center has any information, they know where to reach me."

"You're a brave girl. See you in the morning."

When she tried to call Mike and Julie, there was only a recording to say that service was out of order in the area. They hoped to have temporary service restored within the week.

Karyn couldn't wait to get into the tub for a relaxing bath and pile into bed. How good it was to be home after such exhausting days. The last three days seemed like an eternity when she thought about all that had transpired.

It felt wonderful to submerge herself in a tub full of warm bath water, fragrant with her favorite Charisma bubble bath. She tried to analyze the feelings of numbness that plagued her when she thought about Jim. She wanted desperately to believe he was still alive because he had been a good friend. While listening intently to each survivor who had related their personal loss to her, she had silently shared the depth of their pain. *Is my feeling for Jim really that much different than what I felt for others who are missing? What's the matter with me, anyway?* Shaking her head as if to shake off the question that troubled her, she stepped out of the tub and began to quickly dry herself.

Climbing into her own bed was pure luxury. She switched off the bedside lamp and stretched out to relax. Two seconds later she was sound asleep.

The alarm jarred her awake, and she quickly reached out to shut if off. For a few seconds, a strange feeling crept over her when she realized it was Tuesday morning, and she was back in her own bedroom. She stretched and yawned, luxuriating in the warmth and comfort of her own surroundings. Reluctant to leave the familiar security of the room with its warm peach walls, off-white carpeting, and turquoise accents, she stared at avocado, cream, and turquoise satin-striped swivel chair in the corner of the room. *How would I feel if suddenly everything I owned was washed down the river?* She stared off into space while personalizing the grim thought.

Reality hit her in full force when she thought about getting back to a scheduled routine. She eased out of bed, unfolding one muscle at a time, and started to get ready for work.

✤ ✤ ✤

Business for the day piled up, with subcontractors coming in with bids for the new development before the City Planning Board. Like a walking zombie, Karyn mechanically went through the motions of doing what she needed to do, and yet felt slightly removed from it all.

After what seemed a long workday, she stopped to pick up the mail that had been collecting in her mailbox for the last few days. Going through the contents on the counter, she was interrupted when the phone rang.

"How was your day?" asked Cindy, with an edge of concern in her voice.

"I managed to get through it, but I'm glad it's over. Wade was good to screen some of the calls so I could concentrate on what needed to be done first."

"How did it go with Jim's parents?"

"Mom and Dad went over to talk to them last night. Mom said they were grief stricken. They had lots of questions about what happened. They made plane reservations to fly out early this morning."

"So now what?"

"I didn't mention this to you yesterday because I needed to sort it all out. Eric asked to take me out to dinner tonight."

"You mean the Eric who was on the rafting trip? How did that happen?" Cindy's voice dripped with surprise and curiosity.

"He flew the helicopter that brought us in from the canyon."

"There must be some reason he keeps popping up in your life. Karyn! I can't believe it!"

"I know. I can hardly believe it myself. He was so concerned that I had not heard anything about Jim. He is just such a nice, caring guy. I suppose that's why I accepted the invitation. It doesn't make much sense, does it? In the light of everything else, nothing seems logical right now."

"Karyn, just go out and forget about the last few days."

"I'd better get off the phone, or I won't be ready when he comes to pick me up. Talk to you later." Karyn sighed with resignation as she started for the shower.

Standing nervously in front of her closet surveying the wardrobe within, Karyn finally chose a sleeveless navy sheath with a white over-the-shoulder collar bordered with lace. Stepping into navy pumps, she stood before the mirror to slip on white earrings.

With flushed face, and trembling hands, she thought of the evening ahead. *Why am I so nervous? This will probably be one of those casual dates, and he will fly off to California, never to be heard from again. How can I even think about going out with someone when I don't even know if Jim is dead or alive?* The thought didn't quell the anticipation she felt at seeing Eric again.

He rang the doorbell promptly at seven, dressed in gray slacks, a navy sport coat, light blue shirt, and a stripped tie. Smiling, he greeted her warmly, exuding a quiet confidence.

"You look well-dressed for a pilot who was called out on emergency relief," commented Karyn, as she invited him in.

"A rescue mission wasn't exactly what I had in mind when I packed my flight bag for Colorado. I was actually supposed to be on vacation, so I had dress clothes. Lucky for me. You look terrific! I'd hate to be dressed in my flight clothes and take such a lovely lady our for the evening."

The Charco Broiler was filled with a noisy crowd waiting in line to be seated. The rustic, western atmosphere, combined with the casual diners, helped to put Eric and Karyn at ease as they tried to converse over the noise.

During dinner, Eric's eyes lingered on Karyn's delicate

features. He could not get over how beautiful she looked. Even though he had found her attractive before, tonight she was radiant. The dark circles were gone from beneath her eyes, and her makeup glowed with a clean, fresh look. A natural flush to her cheeks and a rosy-red lip color outlined full, well-shaped lips. The reflection from the overhead lighting made her hair look blue-black, curling softly at her shoulders to frame an ivory complexion.

Karyn looked up from the table several times to catch Eric staring at her. She said something to him, pulling his mind back to their conversation. The evening had gone smoothly, with few moments when it seemed an effort to keep the dialogue flowing. Eric was charming and articulate. Both of them intentionally avoided discussing the sadness of the last few days. Karyn asked about Eric's family.

"I came from a family of pilots with a love for flying. I soloed my senior year in high school. Since then I have been flying everything I could get my hands on. What did you always dream of doing with your life?"

"Early on, I discovered a passion and a talent for art. I've dreamed of becoming a free lance artist. I'm not sure at this point where my degree in Art and Design will take me, but hopefully it will support my desire to see some of the world and paint what I see," smiled Karyn.

A faint light twinkled in the depths of Eric's clear blue eyes. "Ambitious, aren't you? Why in the world are you working for a contractor? It doesn't seem to complement your field."

"In a way it does. I have been able to offer some advice on changes in house plans from a woman's point of view, and I do a lot of decorating for the show homes on some of the developments. When Wade has open houses, he often asks me to show them on weekends. That's the exciting part. A well-decorated, finished product is really a work of art."

Conversation hit a momentary lull, and Eric looked at his watch. "I can't believe it's so late. The steak has been exceptionally good, and my dinner partner delightful. The time has gone all too quickly. However, I'd better take you home," Eric said, as he looked across the table at Karyn. "I need to catch the shuttle to Denver early in the morning. Otherwise, I'll miss my California flight," he said, rising from the table.

When Eric drove up to the condo, he looked thoughtful. "I didn't want to tell you this earlier because I thought it might spoil our evening. They were bringing in more bodies from the canyon this afternoon. You should know something in the next day or two. It's going to be difficult to identify some because of the abrasion from the river and other factors. They will probably have to ask you to identify Jim. I thought you should be prepared for that."

Tears came to Karyn's eyes as Eric spoke. Parking the car, he turned her face gently toward him. "I'm sorry," he said. Taking a handkerchief from his breast pocket, he gently wiped the tears away that trickled down Karyn's cheeks. Then he lifted her chin, and gently kissed her on the lips. "Karyn, I want to see you again, but I can't promise when. In the meantime, will you write to me?"

Karyn nodded her head because she couldn't trust her voice to speak.

The summer night was filled with familiar sounds as Eric walked Karyn to the door. Putting his arms around her, he gently pulled her close. His eyes searched hers in the moonlight, and he saw hers were full of tears. He kissed her…just the briefest kiss. There was no resistance. He kissed her again, maybe just to prove the first hadn't been a mistake. Releasing her, he said, "It's been a wonderful evening that I won't soon forget. I'll drop you a note when I get back to California. Okay?"

Karyn found it hard to think clearly, struggling between two conflicting emotional responses: a sense of loyalty to Jim, and a strong attraction to Eric. His first kiss had turned her emotional equilibrium topsy-turvy. Finding her voice, she answered softly, "I'll look forward to hearing from you. Thanks, Eric, for everything. You've been wonderful."

Chapter 13

A Time to Grieve

Karyn walked into the reception area the next morning and saw Wade already seated at his desk, a pile of invoices before him. He stepped out of his office with his coffee cup, and asked, "Are you sure you're ready to come back to work?"

"It seems the best thing to do right now. It may be days before I hear anything about Jim. At this point, I know it's doubtful that he's alive. I just can't sit around waiting."

Wade filled his coffee cup, and poured one for Karyn. "Cream or sugar?" he asked.

Karyn smiled. I've been working in his office for two years and he doesn't know I always drink my coffee black. She understood he was a successful promoter, but normally not a sensitive person. When she had first started working for him, this had bothered her. As she grew to appreciate his business acumen, she became more tolerant to his lack of sensitivity. They worked together well because her warm friendliness complemented his business demeanor. Wade was fortunate to have his wife to compensate for his cool relationships with other people in social situations.

Karyn was in the middle of balancing the July bank statement when the telephone rang. "Karyn, this is Jenny. I hate to bother you at work, but I thought you should know they brought in a body that might be Jim. They will need you to make a positive identification since his family members have not arrived yet. I'm sorry to have to give you the bad news."

Dazed by the message, Karyn could not control her voice to reply. The tears came in spite of the fact she was trying to maintain her composure. Leaving her desk, she went to the bathroom to let the shock and finality of the news wash over her.

The telephone rang twice, and she could hear Wade picking up the call. It was Jenny, alarmed that Karyn hung up with no response. Wade came and tapped on the bathroom door. "Karyn, are you all right?"

Stepping out, she replied, "Not really. They just called to say they think they brought in Jim's body, and they want me to come over to identify him," she said, drying her eyes with a tissue.

"I'll call Helen. She can go with you." Wade walked back into his office and reached for the phone to call home.

❖ ❖ ❖

"We found Jim in his silver Porsche, buried in a wash, and the car filled to the brim with silt. The key was in the ignition, and the car was apparently running when it was swept away," said the coroner. He pulled back the sheet to allow Karyn to view the face.

Karyn's face turned dead white. She nodded her head, confirming it was Jim.

"I'm sorry, young lady." The gray-haired coroner, in his white coat and gloved hands, looked sympathetically into her tear-filled eyes. "We checked the I.D. in his billfold, and the license plates on the vehicle were registered to him. What do you want to do with his personal belongings?"

A suffocating sensation tightened her throat. "I'll have to

notify his parents…they're planning to fly out today. They'll want to make arrangements to take care of his things."

Peering at Karyn's stricken face, Helen put her arm around her. Karyn's shoulders shook with sobs as Helen guided her from the temporary morgue.

"I'm sorry you had to do that. I know how hard it must be for you."

Helen and Karyn sat in the car for a few minutes, both speechless. Neither woman was prepared for the shock of seeing Jim's lifeless body.

"It's so awful, I can hardly believe it's true," said Karyn. She dried her eyes with a tissue and dabbed at the dark, wet track from her mascara. "The worst part will be having to let Jim's parents know. They wanted to come out immediately…but after Mom told them how difficult things were at the rescue center…they decided to wait and come today."

When Helen turned off the ignition in the parking lot of the condo complex, Karyn invited her in. "I'll fix us some tea."

Karyn moved mechanically from cupboard to stove, making the tea. While they lingered at the table, she related the panic she felt while driving up the canyon on the night of the flood.

"It was raining so hard we could barely see the road at times." Skimming over the details, and shivering with a chill that had nothing to do with the temperature, she recalled the events of the time spent on the mountain. Karyn seemed to momentarily drift away when she described the terror and uncertainty, the blackness of the night as she stumbled up the cliff, and the grief all the survivors experienced while witnessing such violence of nature.

"After feeling totally isolated as I climbed up the mountain, you can't imagine the relief I felt at seeing the light from Jake's flashlight and the group in the meadow. We sat huddled together, cold and wet, wondering what had happened to friends and family members of people living in the canyon. The days at the rescue center were agonizing. We watched the reports come in for families desperately hoping for good news, but having to cope with grief and loss. I will never forget the agony, the blank looks, and the horror on their faces when the reality of their loss hit them in full force."

"The news accounts on TV were shocking. Wade and I kept wondering where you were as we continued listening to the reports."

"With all the trauma at the rescue center, it was almost impossible to call out because of the number of incoming calls."

"Now, Karyn, I don't want you to worry about anything at the office. I'll fill in for you until you feel like coming back to work," said Helen, carrying her cup and saucer to the sink.

After Helen left, Karyn called Jim's parents. They were ready to catch a plane. There was no way to soften the message of their son's tragic death. Karyn hung up the phone and sat staring out the window, seeing nothing. Her mind was whisked away to the events of the last few days. Her head pounded, and she couldn't remember when she had been so physically and emotionally drained. She felt like an apathetic shell, incapable of feeling. Going to the medicine chest, she reached for the aspirin bottle, took two, and climbed into bed.

It was late afternoon before Karyn was aroused from a troubled sleep. The telephone on her bedside table rang. It was Cindy on the line. "Do you feel up to company and a pizza this evening?" She had stopped by the relief station and had seen Jim's name on the list of deceased who had been identified.

"I'll be lousy company, but come by. Give me time to get showered and dressed. I look a wreck."

"I'll pick up the pizza and be there in an hour. Okay?"

Karyn stood beneath the pulsing jets of water, letting them beat the tenseness out of her body. She put on some makeup and pulled on jeans and a T-shirt. The simple activity made her feel better.

She was assembling a salad when Cindy rang the doorbell.

Seated at the bar, eating pizza and salad, Cindy commented, "For a casual friendship, you are taking this pretty hard. Are you sure you didn't love Jim?"

Karyn thought a moment and replied, "I've had time to evaluate our relationship, and I can honestly say that we were just good friends. Jim was fun to be with and generous to a fault with his money. We had many good times together, but I could never imagine us in a serious relationship. He just didn't have the kind of spiritual values that are important to me. The hardest part about the whole thing is the terrible way he died. I'll never forget that night as long as I live. And then to have to identify his body...was a horrible nightmare." Choking back a sob, Karyn covered her eyes with her hands in an effort to blank out the memory of Jim's lifeless form.

Drying her eyes on the back of her hands, she continued. "Jim was a friend, and I don't think he could have been more than that to me. Sometimes I wonder how our relationship lasted for six months. Maybe I wasn't really looking for a serious relationship. Cindy, seeing you go through the experience of losing someone you really loved and cared about was rather frightening. You expected to spend the rest of your life with Tad, and he turned out to be a jerk. I'm not sure I could go through that."

"I kept asking myself how someone who is a Christian could do that to me," said Cindy, shaking her head. "Time has helped me to be more objective about it. What if I had married Tad? Maybe our marriage wouldn't have survived."

"Didn't you feel like the Lord was leading you at the time? Tad always sounded so wonderful from your letters."

"Now I can say that it must not have been the Lord's will, even though I thought it was at the time. In fact, if I had married Tad, I probably wouldn't be here eating pizza with you right now. When I look back, I feel the Lord has a purpose in my being here. Strange, isn't it?"

"I'm so glad you are," said Karyn, as she dried her eyes. "I have to meet Jim's parents at their motel tomorrow morning. How I dread having to try to explain what happened that night. They will be here for a few days to take care of Jim's things. Pray that I'll know what to say to them. What if they hate me for leaving Jim?"

"Oh, Karyn. I don't envy you that job, but I know the Lord will give you special wisdom in dealing with them. You know I'll be praying for you," she said, reaching for Karyn's hand. "It's getting late, and I'd better get home. I have a busy day at work tomorrow. It's hard to believe that the rest of life just goes on as normal," said Cindy, as she slid off the bar stool.

"Thanks for coming over. You have been such a dear through this whole thing. I don't know what I would have done without you." Karyn walked Cindy to the door, and they said good night.

It was late when Karyn slipped in between cool sheets and started to reach for the lamp to shut off the light. A sense of disquiet about the following day caused her to open the drawer of her nightstand to get her Bible and devotion book. Until that moment, it had not occurred to her that her Bible and suitcase had been washed away in Jim's car. The Bible had been a gift from her grandmother on Karyn's sixteenth birthday. *I will have to ask if they found it among Jim's things.*

Karyn was on automatic pilot for the next few days. She felt lethargic, without energy or direction. Nothing seemed real to her. Jim's parents came to take care of the necessary arrangements. They decided to have a funeral service on Friday to allow his friends in Colorado to pay their last respects.

❖ ❖ ❖

The organ played softly in the mortuary as the funeral attendant ushered Karyn to a seat beside Jim's parents. She sat staring at the voluminous arrangements of flowers flanking the walnut casket with its solid brass fittings. A large spray of white roses fanned out over the top of the polished wood, and a heart of red sweetheart rosebuds nestled in the center of the arrangement. The rich wood bespoke the material blessings that had been bestowed on the last of the Blake's two sons. *How can parents endure that kind of grief?* she asked herself, as she sat viewing the scene before her.

The soloist ended "Sometime We'll Understand," and the minister rose from his seat to stand at the podium.

"We're gathered here today to remember this young man who lost his life in a tragic set of circumstances, but it isn't to him that I speak today. It's to the family that have to endure this tragedy.

"Even though you have suffered one of the most difficult losses to bear, there is hope. Christ came to give us life, not just for this life, but for all eternity. All He asks of us is that we accept that free gift of eternal life that He provided for us by dying on the cross in our place.

"Our Heavenly Father knows what you are going through today because He watched His only Son freely offer Himself as a sacrifice for our sins. It's not His desire that any should perish, but that all might come to know Him, and to share in the joy of spending eternity with Him.

"We all make decisions that sometimes have dire consequences. That's one of life's harsh realities. I'm sure Jim never dreamed of the danger he was in when he made a decision during that last critical moment.

"It's only natural that you will grieve the loss of this son, who was also a friend to many of you. He was young and it may not seem fair to you that he was taken at the prime of his life. The river didn't discriminate between young and old. It's hard to understand the random hand of fate, choosing one life and sparing another. However, you can trust that a loving Heavenly Father has a greater purpose in every event that surrounds our lives.

"My prayer for you today is that in your grief and loss, you will turn to the Lord so He can heal your aching heart."

Jim's mother sobbed silently as the minister shared words to console family and friends.

When the service ended, and Karyn filed past the casket, she blotted the tears from her eyes as she once again viewed Jim's still form. At the door she nodded to the pastor, acknowledging his presence.

"Aren't you the young woman who was with Jim the night the flood occurred? Are you all right?" he asked, casting her a doubtful look.

Karyn nodded, struggling for a grip on reality.

"If there's anything I can do to help, I hope you will feel free to call on me," he said in a quiet, compassionate voice.

When the organ music ended and only the parents remained, Mrs. Blake stepped forward to gaze at her son's body lying in the casket. She could no longer control the grief and anguish of her loss. Sobs wracked her body as she clutched his cold hand resting on his chest and kissed his forehead. She was completely devastated by the loss of her second son. After several moments, Jim's father, tears slipping down his cheeks and no longer able to bear the sight of his wife's grief, forcefully moved her to the door.

Standing quietly outside with the others, Jim's friends serving as pallbearers, stood ready to carry the casket from the mortuary to the hearse.

Reflecting on the night Jim refused to leave his car, Karyn realized how important success and material things were in Jim's philosophy of life. His job with a financial investing firm had made success seem to come easily. He was on his way up, and was doing everything in his power to make that a reality. When she met him, he was taking a speech class to enhance his public speaking abilities. He had already been successful in promoting public seminars for financial investors. He had often said, "Money is not the only motivating force that keeps driving you, but the adrenaline that you get from the feeling of success."

Having met Jim's parents, Karyn had a better understanding of the choice Jim had made which took his life. The things they did and said indicated their materialistic view of life.

It was a relief to Karyn when she put the Blakes on the plane for Chicago. Even though nothing was said to indicate they blamed Karyn in any way for Jim's death, there was a cool reserve when she was with them. She felt excluded from their grief. To see their anguish was like reliving the nightmare all over again for Karyn. When she asked if her Bible was among Jim's things, Mrs. Blake replied, "Yes, it was there, but it was badly damaged and I threw it away."

Her cold response reinforced the sense of guilt Karyn felt about Jim's death. *I wonder if they blame me for leaving Jim instead of insisting he come with me? Could I have done anything that might have persuaded him to leave the car?*

Karyn was at a complete loss to know what to do with herself following the funeral. Time seemed to have stalled. Somehow she had to get through the remainder of the day, and find a way to dull the senses overwhelmed by the tragedies of the past week. To return to an empty condo would only added to the emptiness that paralyzed her. She thought about Cindy, but she was at work, and Karyn realized she was poor company for anyone in her present state. Her mind searched for anything to get away from the thoughts that seems to shadow her daylight hours. Her eyes caught the marquee of University Theater's current attraction, "Dr. Zhivago." Without further deliberation, she turned off College Avenue into the parking area. Anything to escape the torment of remembering. A long sigh escaped her. *Now isn't the time to try to figure it all out.* She silently prayed, *Lord, just help me get through it.*

She took a seat off to one side of the theater, feeling strangely self-conscious sitting alone and hoped the place would quickly darken.

The movie gripped her. Every tragic scene made her feel ultra-sensitive. Silent tears slipped down her cheeks. The beauty of the wintry, Russian countryside — trees coated with ice crystals and window panes like frosted glass were captivating. Loosing herself in someone else's tragedy proved to be a temporary escape from the depressing day.

✤ ✤ ✤

Several days later Karyn thought about the content of Pastor Moore's funeral message. She felt he was a pastor she could relate to. Her infrequent visits to church on special occasions had been nice, but left her missing her home church and the pastor who had been a constant influence in her life. She knew she needed to find a church home in this area.

On Sunday morning, she slipped into a pew at Foothills Bible Church and realized the effort was more difficult than Karyn had imagined. She felt like a stranger.

Pastor Moore's sermon centered on the passage of Jesus' compassion for His disciples when they failed to understand the real purpose of His ministry. Karyn soon forgot about the surroundings as she thoughtfully concentrated on the message. The organ music and the choir added a sense of familiarity when they sang some of Karyn's favorite hymns. The soloist had a clear, bell-like quality to her voice as she sang, "Because He Lives." The song seemed to be sung just for her benefit.

At the close of the service, several of the members introduced themselves to Karyn. There was genuine friendliness in their expressions of welcome.

Pastor Moore and his wife stood in the foyer to greet parishioners following the morning service. When he recognized Karyn, he was quick to say, "I'm so glad you were able to come this morning. I want you to meet my wife Marty." Turning to his wife, he said, "Karyn lost a friend in the flood. I had the funeral service for the young man."

Marty paused to look solicitously at Karyn. "I'm so sorry to hear that," she said, taking Karyn's hand in both of hers. "Sometimes it helps to be able to talk about a tragedy like that.

Would you mind if we came to visit with you sometime this week?"

Karyn, impressed with Marty's warmth and the compassion expressed in the attractive woman's eyes, replied, "That would be nice."

"We'll be sure to call before we come," said Marty. "We need to check our schedule with the church secretary first to see what day might work out best."

"I'll give you my home phone and also my work number," said Karyn. She searched through her purse for a small notebook.

Pastor Moore, pen ready in hand, quickly wrote the phone numbers down on the back of one of his church calling cards.

It was Saturday afternoon when Pastor Moore and Marty came to call. Karyn had baked some fresh sugar cookies and served steaming cups of coffee in the living room.

"Karyn, tell us what happened the night up the canyon. Jim's parents related very little of the details when they made the funeral arrangements with me," said Pastor Moore. "I got the distinct impression they weren't very comfortable in a church environment."

"I'm sure they weren't. Jim told me his family rarely went to church. They always had too many social events on their calendar."

"I understand you and Jim were on your way to visit friends for the weekend when Jim was caught in the flood."

Karyn found it easy to relate the tragic circumstances to the Moores. They listened attentively without interrupting her. Occasionally she stopped, struggling to maintain her composure as she recounted the details. When she concluded, she looked up at the two people sitting on the sofa in front of her, sympathy written on their faces. Karyn suddenly realized how easy it would have been to bury all the nightmarish details deep within her, and then have them resurrected, unbidden, at another time.

"Karyn, I sense you're carrying a load of guilt about Jim's death. Now let's think about this...what could you have actually done to prevent his death? Died with him?

"Jim made a choice you aren't responsible for. A sad choice, but nevertheless, it was his choice. God doesn't hold you responsible for that choice, and though you may feel some guilt about it, you are not responsible for his death."

Pastor Moore continued, "It's tragic that so many people lost their lives in the flood. We can't begin to understand what God's purpose was in that, but nothing happens aside from His divine purpose. Do you suppose there was anything good that came out of that tragedy?"

Marty spoke up. "We are constantly hearing people who witness to the fact that because their lives were spared, they know God has a purpose for them in this life. They had never given God much credit for anything prior to this."

Nodding his head in agreement, while he turned the pages in his Bible, Pastor Moore continued. "Karyn, do you remember the verse in Romans 8:28 that says, 'All things work together for good to those that love the Lord'?" In his deep resonant voice he read the verse aloud. "We have to take that by faith because in our human mind we can never comprehend it. God's ways often puzzle us, but some day we'll understand His ultimate purpose in everything He does."

Looking at his watch, he said, "We must go now, but first I want to pray that God will give you His peace as you recall the events of that night." Concluding the moving prayer, he and Marty rose to thank Karyn for the refreshments.

"Thank you so much for coming," said Karyn. She walked them to the door, her eyes glistening with tears.

Marty put her arms around Karyn and said, "The Lord always knows how to comfort us. He often sends someone around to give us a hug when we most need it."

The hot days of August plodded on. Some days, just to get out of bed proved to be an effort. Karyn rose to meet the necessary details of the day, but she hardly felt refreshed as she normally would from a pleasant night's sleep.

The next week passed, the birds sang and the sun arose every morning, despite all that had happened. The days took on a semblance of normality. Wade asked Karyn to meet Helen at the highrise to do a walk-through of the completed, upscale apartments for a final inspection before the first tenants moved in.

"First, I particularly want to see the manager's apartment after the carpenter installed the cupboards," said Helen. They walked down the hall of the first floor, footsteps muffled by the plush carpeting. The smell of new carpeting and fresh paint greeted their nostrils when they entered the apartment. The custom walnut cabinets gleamed with the finishing touch of a craftsman's talent. Karyn smiled with pleasure as she ran her hand over the beautiful grain of the wood, and opened the drawers and cupboard doors to inspect the interiors.

"Let's check the carpet and draperies in Dr. Larson's apartment," said Karyn, closing the door to the unit. They walked down the hall to the elevator and pushed the button to the penthouse on the fourth floor. Karyn commented, "The movers will be delivering his furniture tomorrow."

Satisfied that the decorators had achieved the harmony the upscale rental demanded, and the cleaning people had left the unit spotless, Karyn felt a sense of relief the job was finished.

A tired sigh escaped her as she climbed into her car. It occurred to her she had left some things at the cleaners two weeks ago and had failed to pick them up. She made a stop at the cleaners and drove to Steele's Market to buy some groceries to restock her refrigerator and cupboard.

Karyn walked into the store, looking over her shopping list, anxious to quickly get what she needed. She pondered at the meat counter and finally chose a small package of chicken breasts and a beef roast. Walking to the produce department, she picked up a head of lettuce and turned to find a bag to put it in. A faint whiff of Preferred Stock cologne caused her to turn around as someone walked by her. Startled by the fragrance that reminded her of Eric, she glanced up to see the form of a tall, blond man who was selecting grapefruit at the fruit counter. Even though it couldn't possibly be Eric, she found herself going to the counter to pick up two grapefruit. The young man smiled as they shared the same space. He really looked nothing like Eric, but his scent and form brought a sharp poignant memory surfacing to Karyn's mind.

At the mailbox, she picked up her mail on the way into the house. When she thumbed through several pieces of mail, she noticed a return address from California. Eric had sent her a letter! She quickly opened it. She was both surprised and pleased to hear from him.

Dear Karyn,

As per my promise, I'm writing and anxiously awaiting your reply. Have you had any information about Jim? From the news, I see the casualty list of identified victims is mounting. We get only sketchy parts of news here. How are you doing?

I still can't get over the shock of seeing you when we landed the chopper in the mountains. I had planned to look you up when I got back to Fort Collins again. Little did I dream it would be in that kind of situation.

I'm glad you agreed to have dinner with me, even though it must have seemed like a strange invitation at such a bizarre time.

It sounds like I'm in for a transfer very soon. Wish it could be Lowry Air Force Base in Denver, but I'm afraid that isn't what they have in mind. My address will remain the same until I know what the score is.

Take care of yourself.

Eric

It was several days before Karyn sat down to reply to Eric's letter. What should I say to him? He walked into my life again when everything seemed at its very worst, and yet, he was understanding and thoughtful in a way that continued to surprise me. Dinner with him had been exciting and devoid of the kind of awkward moments that sometimes accompany a new relationship.

But do I really want a courtship via letters from a guy whom I might rarely see? What would it be like to see him under other circumstances? She didn't quite trust her own heart in the matter.

Karyn responded with a letter thanking Eric for his concern. It was not easy to relate the facts of Jim's death or to express the numb feelings she continued to have when she thought about how it happened. The letter conveyed her sense of guilt that she had so narrowly escaped death on that fateful night. She thanked him again for dinner and a wonderful evening.

It had been over two weeks since the night of the flood. Karyn was at the office, sitting at the computer reworking a floor plan that Wade had sketched out for one of his prospective clients. The door opened, and in walked Mike and Julie. Karyn was appalled when she realized she had made no effort to contact them in the past week. The two women met midway in the office and warmly embraced.

"We heard about Jim. We're so sorry," said Julie. "There was no way we could get into Fort Collins to check on you. The Highway Department has just finished a temporary road out of the canyon, and until now, we've had to get all our supplies in Estes.

Crews are gradually getting telephone service restored. We've literally been cut off from this area."

Julie looked into Karyn's face. The strain of the last few weeks was clearly visible in the dark lines under her eyes, and her normally smiling eyes were dimmed with sadness. "How are you doing?" she asked in genuine concern.

"It still seems like a bad dream that will go away. Working again has helped to have something else to do besides relive that night. What did you think when we didn't show up?"

"We started dinner without you, expecting that you would be there any time. We had no idea what was going on at first. Mike and the men went down to the river to see who was talking on the bullhorn. That was our first indication of anything unusual happening. Before the night was over, we had twenty people sleeping in our house. They just kept wandering in when they saw our lights. We had candles and lanterns all over the place. The men watched all night to make sure it was safe for us to stay in the cabin. So much water kept coming off the canyon walls we weren't sure it would be wise to stay there. I don't think any of us realized the magnitude of the storm until later."

"Fortunately, we had a good builder, and the cabin was secure," said Mike. "Is Wade in? I have to tell him I'm glad he was my builder. We had no damage to the cabin during the worst of the storm."

Wade stepped to the doorway of his office. "Come on in, Mike."

Julie continued, "We literally ate everything in the house before rescue crews got in to take people out. We were more fortunate than others because our cupboards had been well stocked for our weekend guests, or we might have all gone hungry. The most critical thing was drinking water. Because of the danger of sewage in our water supply, we actually drained the hot water tank for drinking water, and then started boiling tap water.

It was a terrible experience, but nothing compared to what you must have gone through. How did you and Jim get separated?"

Karyn told her briefly what happened up the canyon. Their conversation was interrupted by the telephone.

"We must go, Karyn," said Julie as Mike stepped out of Wade's office. "We wanted to let you know how sorry we were to hear about Jim. We're so glad to know you're safe. Keep in touch now, won't you?"

"Maybe we can have that barbecue again at a later date and under happier circumstances," said Mike.

"What a nightmare!" said Julie. "We are the lucky ones. At least we lived to tell about it!"

Chapter 14

Waiting

When Eric reported back to Beale Air Force Base, he learned he was scheduled to fly secret reconnaissance missions from Mildenhall Air Force Base in England. The missions were highly classified, and security regulations would not permit him to contact his family for the entire period of the mission. He and his flight crew were on their way for intensive training before Karyn's letter reached him.

It had been two months since Karyn had sent a letter to Eric. She was surprised she had not heard from him again. Maybe he was just a nice, caring man who had popped in her life in unusual circumstances. Her intuition told her Eric had been more than mildly interested in her, but maybe he had another commitment in California.

Still feeling lost after Jim's death, Karyn began to realize how comfortable their relationship had become over the previous six months. Since she was preoccupied and busy with her job over the summer, it made it easy for her to decline dates with fellow students. She was relieved for the change of pace when fall classes started again.

School began with the usual heavy assignments. Karyn took a

lighter load for the semester, enabling her to continue her job with Wade Construction and still keep up with the demands of the classroom. The additional practical experience before graduation in the spring would look good on the resumes she had started to send out.

The first morning in her computer-drafting class, she selected a computer that would be assigned to her for the semester. The class soon filled up, and she looked over to see a dark-haired young man take the seat next to her. His curly hair and brown eyes first caught her attention. He stood six feet, with a nice athletic build. Turning to her, he smiled and said, "I hope you didn't have this seat reserved for someone."

Karyn returned the smile and replied, "No, it's a first-come basis. It's all yours."

The instructor called the roll to match names to faces. Her seatmate answered to the name of Terry Hughs. After hearing Karyn's name called, he turned to her, extended his hand and said, "Hello, Karyn." His smile radiated a natural friendliness.

As Karyn gathered up her book and assignments for the semester, Terry commented, "It looks like this will be an interesting class. So what's your major? Why are you taking computer drafting?"

Karyn and Terry started walking out of the classroom together. "My major is Art and Design, but I'm working for a construction company. Computer drafting has so many advantages in the building field. Why are you taking the course?"

"I have a mechanical engineering degree. I'm taking some additional courses, at my companies expense, to get into research and development. I have an idea for a beet harvesting machine operated by computer." The conversation continued until they reached the parking lot and headed in opposite directions.

September had rolled into October, and Karyn and Terry began seeing each other frequently. Often, they met after class in the snack bar for coffee to discuss assignments and problems in the course.

One Friday afternoon after class, Terry said, "There's a good movie in town. Do you have big plans for tonight?"

"Not particularly. Sounds fun. You buy the theater tickets, and I'll treat you for the hamburgers afterwards. Is it a deal?"

"I'll pick you up at six-thirty," Terry said, "but you have to tell me where."

Karyn jotted her address on a piece of paper from her notebook and handed it to Terry. While she was writing, Terry found himself measuring the top of her head to his shoulder. He liked to be taller than the women he dated. Karyn was just right.

"See you later," said Karyn. She heard Terry whistling as they started for their cars.

Karyn felt a mixture of emotions as she drove home. Jim's death made her feel a little guilty about dating someone else. *What should I be feeling? Who makes the rules? Am I going to have a good time or feel guilty? Is it wrong to have some feelings for someone who is alive instead of dead? How will I feel about another man in my life right now?* With Eric it had been different. The tragedy of the flood had seemed to temporarily meld the two of them together. Karyn knew he would be leaving, and she might never hear from him again. Recalling the events of the summer was like having lived another life in some past history, and yet she hadn't been able to completely detach herself from that life.

Terry arrived at her door saying, "I hope you like suspense movies. "The French Connection" with Gene Hackman is in town, and I'm anxious to see it. Is that okay with you?"

"Just as long as there's nothing about floods in the movie," Karyn commented.

Terry looked at her in surprise. "Why do you say that?"

"No real reason," Karyn replied, trying to make light of her comment. The pain was still too real for her to try to explain her flickering emotions to someone she scarcely knew.

Terry proved to be an entertaining and intelligent date. Karyn enjoyed the movie and the verbal exchange while they lingered at Around the Corner long after they finished their hamburgers. Their mutual interest in classroom subjects, teachers, and what the future held kept the conversation stimulating.

When Terry walked her to the door, Karyn felt a rise of apprehension. *Is he going to expect me to kiss him good night?* Karyn turned to thank him for the evening, and Terry reached out to put his arms around her to draw her closer. As he did, he could feel the tension in Karyn's body. "What's the matter? Don't you kiss on the first date? This is our first real date, you know."

"It's not that, Terry. I had a wonderful time this evening. It has nothing to do with you."

"Okay, as long as I didn't do something to offend you." Terry released her, and said, "I had a good time, too, so let's do this again."

❖ ❖ ❖

Karyn found herself counting the months since she had last heard from Eric. *Was he just someone to talk to who understood how I was really feeling? Or did we have another connection other than the circumstances that brought us together?*

The telephone ringing on her counter startled her as she sat at her drawing board concentrating on a project for a class assignment. She was surprised to hear Eric's voice when she picked up the receiver. "Karyn, I'm in Denver for a few days. May I come and see you while I'm here?"

"Of course. It's such a surprise to hear from you! What are your plans?"

"I have a few days leave before I have to report for duty again. I'm sorry I didn't get around to answering your letter sooner. I was on special assignment, and your letter arrived after I left. During training we weren't allowed to contact anyone."

"Sounds very important and very secretive," Karyn whispered into the phone, just for emphasis. She tried to sound interested, without divulging her disappointed in not hearing from him.

"How would you like to go skiing Saturday? I thought I could come to Fort Collins Friday night, and we could have dinner. Then we could get an early start for Winter Park on Saturday morning, and get in a full day of skiing."

"It sounds wonderful. The snow should be great this weekend. They just had four inches of fresh powder last night."

"I'll give you a call when I get into town on Friday. So much has happened since I saw you this past summer, and we have a lot of catching up to do. We can talk about it over dinner."

Karyn was elated. Emotions she had tried to bury came flooding back. *I can't tell my heart to stop caring,* she thought, sitting at her drawing board staring into space. Trying to concentrate on the project before her became a futile effort. Finally, she threw her pencil and ruler aside, and decided to go running in the park near her condo. Maybe the crisp air would clear her brain.

Light snow continued to fall, giving the world a white, unbroken serenity. Karyn's breath left a faint mist as she ran around the park, breaking a fresh trail in the powdery snow. Her heart felt as light as the snowflakes falling around her.

❖ ❖ ❖

Eric rang the doorbell as Karyn sprayed a fragrant mist of cologne at her neckline. When she opened the door, her heart raced, and she was flushed with excitement. Eric stood there, tall and handsome, flashing her a smile. Whatever reservations she might have had about their meeting again evaporated like rain clouds dispelled by the sun. It had been a long four months since she had last seen him.

"I'll Be Seeing You" was playing softly in the background as they walked into the Wine Cellar for dinner. The hostess guided them to a quiet table in the corner. "That song has been playing in my mind since we met last summer," said Eric. He began to hum along with the melody.

"You have a nice voice. I'd love to hear you sing the entire song."

"Sometime I might, but right now I don't even know all the words. Isn't it strange how many songs there are that we really like, but we'd never pass a test if we had to sing the complete song. That one I'll have to memorize for you," said Eric.

Karyn smiled, "I'll consider that a promise."

They finished dinner and lingered over coffee and dessert. Eric said, "I feel really remiss about not writing to you since this summer. Our Air Force training for special assignments has been intense. Once we complete the training, and the Air Force sends us out on a mission, we have no contact with anyone except the officers we deal with. The rest of life just gets put on hold...not because I want it that way. It's just what the job demands of us. Does that make sense to you?"

"Is it because you love flying so much, or is it the secrecy of the mission?" Karyn asked, as she tried to understand.

"I think it is both. Our flying schedule is very demanding, but when you love what you're doing, all else becomes of secondary importance. Now that I'm here with you, this suddenly becomes important." Eric reached over for Karyn's hand resting beside her coffee cup, taking in at a glance her hands with well manicured nails.

The warm intimacy of Eric's touch sent tingling sensations up Karyn's arm, distracting her momentarily from what he was saying.

"As soon as I got back to the states, I knew I had to see you again."

Karyn tried to interpret the look in Eric's eyes. He was looking intently at her, making her slightly uncomfortable. He seemed to be reading her mind, and she wasn't sure she wanted to be that transparent at this moment. *I've never fallen in love before and I don't know how it might feel to be rejected by someone I really cared about. Is this just an amusement to fill in the space of a few days vacation time?*

"How are you doing after everything that happened this summer," asked Eric.

"It was pretty traumatic for a while. For several weeks, I felt like a programmed robot. Going back to work was like stepping into a different world. It was strange to see people doing normal things like shopping and strolling along the streets. It took several months before I could really believe that life could be normal again. My friends were great to help me through the worst of it. For one thing, they wouldn't let me dwell on the feelings of grief and loss. However, experiencing that much heartache and tragedy changed my whole perspective on life."

"I could never quite understand your relationship to Jim. You seemed so caught up in what happened to him. Did you love the guy?"

"We were good friends. At times, I wondered if I could love him, but the relationship just didn't have the shooting sparks I think real love should have. As I think about our friendship now, we were two people with totally different values."

"I know. There have been several times I thought this was it, but it didn't take me long to realize I didn't love this person as much as my flying."

Karyn smiled at the analogy, even though it expressed something she had feared might be true of Eric. His words seemed to hang in the air as if for inspection.

Eric broke the moment of silence. "How early shall we start for the slopes tomorrow? Is seven o'clock too early for you? If we can get up there by nine-thirty, we'll get in a good day of skiing. I have to catch a plane out of Denver early Sunday morning."

Karyn tried to conceal her disappointment, even though she knew he was on a short leave.

As Eric helped her out of the car at the condo, Karyn asked, "Would you like another cup of coffee before you go back to your motel?"

"I'd love one." Eric didn't need another cup of coffee, but he felt reluctant to say good night.

The air was crisp and the snow crunched underfoot as Eric walked Karyn to her door. A pale moon hung overhead, accentuated by the blackness of the night.

The breakfast bar in Karyn's kitchen was covered with her drafting plans, spread out where she had been working.

"Oh, this is what you do in your spare time after work, classes, and dating the men in your life."

"I'm working on a class assignment. This is a renovation drawing that updates an older home to create the most livable space. I'm having trouble with the area where I need to put the laundry facilities."

"Why don't you just build on a room?" laughed Eric.

"That would be too easy. We have to make the changes within the current structure."

Eric leaned over for a closer look at the plans, sat down on the barstool, and proceeded to make some suggestions. His shoulder brushed hers and Karyn was acutely aware of his presence and the faint aroma of his aftershave. She could feel the erratic beat of her heart.

Struggling to concentrate, Karyn responded, "Those are good ideas." She began moving her ruler to measure the distance in the kitchen area where Eric had suggested. Both bent over the plans, heads almost touching. Eric reached over and touched Karyn's chin to turn her face around. He planted a gentle kiss on her lips. His voice was husky when he said, "Let's build this one for us."

There was no way Karyn could reply. Eric was giving her another long, lingering, good night kiss.

Chapter 15

Rivals

The ski slopes at Winter Park were crowded with weekend skiers. Eric was an excellent skier, and Karyn only relatively good for lack of practice.

Eric proved to be patient and attentive while Karyn got the feel of the slopes once again.

"That's four runs on Mary Jane this morning. I'm ready for lunch. How about you?" Eric asked, as they came down the slope to the ski lodge.

"More than ready," replied Karyn. She kicked out of her skis and stomped her boots several times to warm her cold feet.

After lunch, they made a couple of runs on the more difficult ski slopes. The blue sky became zinc-gray, and the wind blew puffs of snow into their faces. Snowflakes began to leave patterns on their clothing and dust their eyelashes as they reached the bottom of the ski run.

"Why don't we make another run, and find a good restaurant

for dinner?" asked Eric.

"It's been fun, but I can't make another trip up the slope. I was about to suggest that you go without me this time."

"I don't want to do that." Eric gave her a questioning glance.

"I insist," said Karyn, her nose and cheeks red from the cold. "I'm going into the lodge to get warm, and get something hot to drink. You may not have another opportunity to ski very soon, but I will."

"Are you sure you don't mind?" asked Eric, a dubious expression on his face.

"Not at all. I'm really too cold. It doesn't sound like fun at this point."

Karyn stood her skis and poles into the rack and turned to watch Eric catch the chair lift. Stamping the snow from her boots, she turned to walk into the lodge. While she was standing in line at the cafeteria, she heard someone call her name. Karyn turned to see Terry coming toward her with a very pleased smile on his face. "Why didn't you tell me you were going to be here this weekend? We could have come up together, or are you with someone?"

"I came up with a friend. He decided to take another run up the hill, and I came in to get warm," she said, pulling off her gloves and throwing back her fur-trimmed parka.

Karyn paid the cashier and picked up her cup of hot cider, feeling the warmth permeating her cold hands. She waited for Terry to get his order of fries and coffee. He motioned her to a table where his friends had gathered and made introductions around the table. They laughed and exchanged banter about their adventures on the slope. Finally, one of the men pushed back his chair. "Karyn, it's nice to meet you. If you and Terry will excuse us, we're headed back to the slope to get in some more skiing."

"You have a great group of friends, Terry," said Karyn, as the men made their way out.

"These are guys I work with at the office, and we planned this trip for a day when we could all get together. Now, where have you been keeping yourself? I haven't seen much of you lately.

Worse yet, I feel like you have been avoiding me." Barely disguising the hurt, he said, "What do I need to do to straighten this out?" He looked intently at her, waiting for a reply.

"Terry, honestly, it's nothing you've done as I told you before. I had something very traumatic happen to me last summer, and I haven't really felt like I wanted to explain it to anyone. It has nothing to do with you personally. Actually, if I seem to have been avoiding you, it's because I've had a busy schedule with work and school. In fact, next weekend Wade asked me to host an open house in one of his new housing developments. It gives me very little time for the computer work I need to do at school for our next assignment, and I have an essay due for an art history class. Forgive me, okay?"

"I didn't mean to pry, but I had to know if you were ever going to let me take you out again," said Terry, looking at her with a very serious expression on his face.

When Eric walked into the lodge, he saw Karyn seated across from Terry. From the intense look on Terry's face, the conversation appeared to be a serious one. Eric's first reaction was pure green jealousy. *Get a handle on yourself. You don't own her.* When Eric approached them, Terry looked up.

"Hi," Eric said casually, not quite certain whether he should interrupt.

Karyn turned at the sound of Eric's voice. "Eric, I want you to meet Terry Hughs. Terry and I have been in the same computer class this last semester."

Terry stood to shake hands with Eric. "Nice to meet you, Eric.

The calm demeanor of the trio belied the tension they felt while each one tried to think of something to say to relieve the awkwardness of the moment.

"I hate to break and run, but my buddies will be wondering what happened to me. See you in class, Karyn." Terry flashed her a smile that was not only sexy, but dangerously charming.

"I hope I didn't interrupt something," Eric said, sending Karyn a questioning glance. Terry's expression had not been that of a casual acquaintance.

Karyn merely shook her head, not quite sure how to answer at that moment.

Snow fell in huge, fluffy flakes as Karyn and Eric walked from the lodge, loaded down with skis and poles. The wind had picked up, and the snow swirled around them in the cold crystalline air as they made their way to the car.

"I asked one of the skiers riding the lift with me to recommend the best restaurant in town. He suggested Jerry's Steak and Seafood restaurant, just a couple of blocks from here. He said it's always busy, but it's worth the wait."

A giant moss-rock fireplace across the north wall greeted them when they walked into the lounge.

"That fire looks inviting," said Eric, rubbing his gloved hands together and guiding Karyn to a sofa. "You get comfortable while I check to see how long we might have to wait for a table."

Guests came to the door, stomping the snow from their boots, and exhaling moist air into the gathering dusk. The room vibrated with the sound of enthusiastic diners, lending a holiday ambience to the evening.

"We only have a twenty-minute wait," said Eric. He sat down beside Karyn, casually putting his arm over the back of the sofa and pulling her closer to him. She snuggled into the crook of his arm, feeling the warmth and closeness of Eric's body. Both of them sat quietly, totally conscious of the other's presence. They stared into the fire, mesmerized by the flames flickering as the fiery tongues sought to consume a log. It fell from the grate to shower live red coals on the concrete below.

For an instant Karyn became the only living thing in the room for him. The intimate moment was interrupted by a waitress calling Eric's name for a table.

"This is such a cozy spot, I could fall asleep right here," Karyn said as she got up, hating to leave the security of nestling in Eric's arm. The butterfly shrimp entree they ordered was done to perfection. While enjoying dinner, they laughed together as they recalled the near accidents on the slope while they adjusted their ski legs.

Karyn remembered Eric's athletic grace as she tried to keep up with him on the tricky ski runs. Watching him intently while he related an amusing incident, Karyn was fascinated by the masculine timbre of his voice, by the blue eyes that smiled across the table at her, and by the square chin with a slight cleft in the center. She felt a compelling need to memorize each detail about him to hold them tightly in her memory. Already, the knowledge that he would soon have to leave brought a growing sense of loss and frustration.

Eric tipped the waiter generously as they left.

The three-hour drive from Winter Park was slow. Traffic crept along because of the snow pack on I-70 into Denver. Eric reached out for Karyn's hand to pull her beside him. She snuggled up close, savoring the moments she had him all to herself. Time took on a new quality...one she had no desire to see end.

Their conversation roamed from one topic to another. Eric talked about his assignments in the Air Force without divulging classified information. He asked Karyn about school, and how her job was working out with a school schedule. He was tempted to ask more about Terry, but decided he would sound like a jealous schoolboy. For the first time in his life, Eric felt at a loss to analyze a little knot of fear growing inside him.

❖ ❖ ❖

It was midnight when Eric took the Fort Collins exit from Interstate 25. Karyn, feeling drowsy from the long day, laid her head back on the seat and closed her eyes momentarily.

"Hey, Sleeping Beauty. Have you got another cup of that good coffee?" asked Eric, as they pulled into the condo parking lot.

Startled, Karyn apologized for drifting into a semi-dreamy state. "Of course," she murmured. "I think we both need a cup of coffee, and I wouldn't think of letting you leave without one on a cold night like this."

Eric came around the car to help Karyn out, putting his arm protectively around her. They faced into the blowing snow swirling around them as they walked up the steps to her door.

"You put the coffee on, and I'll bring in your skis."

Shedding her ski jacket, Karyn started the coffee and went into the living room to put a Glen Miller record on the stereo.

From the kitchen doorway, Eric said, "That's dancing music." Coming up behind Karyn, he pulled her into his arms and began slowly waltzing her around the living room. The fragrance of her perfume was intoxicating. He held her close to his chest, with his nose brushing the side of her hair.

"You're making it very difficult to think about leaving tomorrow, Karyn," said Eric, with an unusual huskiness in his voice. His blue eyes darkened, capturing hers. He stopped dancing and lifted Karyn's chin to plant a long, passionate kiss on her lips. His lips were warm and persuasive. Eric was gripped by feelings he had never felt before. For a mad moment, he even wanted to tell her he loved her.

Karyn's response to his kiss said everything she wanted to tell him, but couldn't put into words. The beating of her heart was so loud she could feel the pounding in her ears. When she looked into Eric's eyes, there was an unspoken message in the way he was looking at her. Unnerved by his nearness, she turned to avoid his eyes, and taking his hand led him to the safety of the kitchen.

When they sat down at the table with their coffee, Eric spoke. "I don't know how long I'll be gone on this next mission, but will you promise to write?"

"Yes, of course. It may be a little like a one-sided conversation," laughed Karyn, "since you may not be able answer my letters."

"I'll call you at the first opportunity I have. I don't want that Terry to turn on too much charm while I'm gone," said Eric, mischief in his eyes, but seriously considering the possibility. It was a simple statement, but there was nothing simple about the way he held her gaze. Reluctantly looking at his watch, he discovered it was well past one o'clock in the morning. Eric made his apologies for having to leave to drive back to Denver. He gave her a kiss that left both of them breathless before he walked out into the night.

Karyn followed him out the front entrance to wave a final goodbye.

At the foot of the stairs leading up to the door, Eric turned to look back at Karyn standing beneath the outside light, the glow casting a halo around her dark hair. He felt a keen sense of loss knowing it might be some time before he would see her again.

Karyn stood on the deck watching, vainly trying to think of some excuse to call him back.

Chapter 16

Distractions

A m I glad to see you!" said Wade, when Karyn walked into the office. "Mrs. Damon is very unhappy with the carpet selection she made for the home they purchased on Centennial Drive. Do you suppose you can help pacify the woman by going over there to see what the problem is?"

"I know what the difficulty is. She insisted on selecting a carpet that had to be dyed to match her draperies. Nothing I could say would convince her it's very difficult to dye to an exact shade. When they rolled the carpet out in her living room, she was surprised at the color. I'll go talk to her and see what we can do to work out the problem." On her way out the door, Karyn grabbed her brief case.

When Karyn rang the bell at the Damon home, she could hear Mrs. Damon's angry voice. Red-faced from her outburst, and hardly in a mood for visitors, she threw open the door.

"These finish carpenters are just making a mess of my wallpaper," she bellowed, ready to vent her hostility on the first available listener. "And I'm not a bit happy with the color of my carpet. I've spent four thousand dollars on draperies, and they don't harmonize with the carpet."

119

"Let me take a look to see what can be done about it," said Karyn, as she put her arm around the distraught woman. "There's definitely a problem," said Karyn. She surveyed the roll of carpeting partially stretched out in the room. "I'll need the carpet sample to take back to the dealer. Since you special ordered the carpet, there might be something wrong with the dye lot. I'll also need your originally dyed sample to take back to the salesman to compare the two pieces."

While Karyn quietly talked to Mrs. Damon, she became more conciliatory. A look of surprise came over the older woman's face and she exclaimed, "You are the same young woman who helped us after the flood! I thought you looked familiar. My husband and I came to the table where you were working at the rescue center. You were so kind and patient, and we were so terribly frightened. It was such a sad time for us," said Mrs. Damon, motioning for Karyn to be seated on the fireplace hearth. "We lost our cabin, two new automobiles we had just purchased, and some of our good neighbors. We were lucky to get out with our lives.

"The evening of the flood my husband remarked how still it was, just like before a storm. Usually the birds are singing and the squirrels are chattering to each other in the yard. Instead, there was an eerie kind of stillness, like a forewarning of something to happen. It seemed like nature tried to tell us of an impending disaster, but we were too busy to pay attention."

Karyn listened quietly while Mrs. Damon related their personal terror. "My husband and I crossed the flooded river holding on to a rope stretched across by the rescue teams. It was terrifying! We were so thankful for those brave men who were making every effort to get all of us out of the lower canyon."

"It was an experience none of us who lived through will ever forget. We were the lucky ones," said Karyn quietly. "No, I should say our guardian angels were watching over us. God must still have some purpose for our lives."

Rising to leave, Karyn patted the woman's shoulder in sympathy and assured Mrs. Damon she would do all she could to resolve the problem with the carpet.

"I'm sorry I was in such bad humor when you arrived," the older woman said, apologetically. "Do come back and have tea with me one of these afternoons," invited Mrs.Damon, in a motherly tone, as she walked Karyn to her car.

❖ ❖ ❖

It was Monday morning at the office, and Karyn checked her calendar for the day. Realizing she needed to contact Mrs. Damon, she dialed her number.

"Mrs. Damon, Karyn Anderson from Wade Construction."

"Yes, Karyn. I've been hoping to hear from you about the carpet."

"When I talked with the carpet salesman, he assured me the original order had been correct. He called the carpet mill in Kansas City, and they had shipped your carpet to the Denver warehouse. That is apparently where the mistake occurred. They'll put your carpet on a truck and it should be here by Wednesday."

"Oh, I'm so glad that we don't have to reorder," sighed Mrs. Damon.

"I'll call the carpet layer again to reschedule and let you know when to expect him. He promised to come back as soon as the carpet is here. I'll be there personally to make sure the order is correct this time, and that everything will be completed as quickly as possible."

"Oh, thank you, Karyn. The movers are coming this Saturday, and I'm having out-of-town guests next week. I wanted every detail completed by the time my guests arrive on Sunday."

Karyn hung up the phone with a sigh of relief. She hated to think they might have had to start the ordering process all over again.

Curled up on the sofa, Karyn tossed a woolen throw over her legs and picked up the current novel she had been reading. She jumped when the phone rang, breaking the silence of the evening.

"Karyn, this is Cathy. I received your lovely birthday card and note, and decided we should get together. Mark has six tickets for the Boulder-CSU game on Saturday. I'm planning an after-game buffet, so bring Terry and meet us at my apartment before the game. I've arranged a blind date for Cindy to meet Mark. I think those two would make a great pair," said Cathy, with emphasis. "I thought it would be safer to make it a six-some in case my match making doesn't work out. Can you make it?"

"I'll check with Terry and get back to you. Sounds great to me," said Karyn. She smiled when she thought about Cindy's normal reaction to blind dates.

The impulse to call Cindy was more than Karyn could stand. "Cindy, I just had a call from Cathy Preston about the CSU-Boulder game on Saturday. So you are going to meet Mark, the doctor. How exciting! Have you talked to him yet?"

"He called me to make the final arrangements. We talked on the phone for quite a while. He sounds really nice. He'll complete his internship this spring and plans to open a pediatric clinic. He's an avid football fan, but dates very little because he's too busy. That's about all I know about him at this point."

"And by the way, Karyn, where have you been? I've been trying to call you for two days," laughed Cindy. "I was beginning to get worried about you."

"Well—Terry and I went skiing over the weekend."

"You and Terry?"

"Don't sound so surprised. After all, you know I haven't heard anything from Eric in ever so long."

"Sorry. I didn't mean to sound judgmental. I'm just surprised."

Quickly changing the subject, Karyn said, "Cindy, I'm so excited for you. If Mark is as nice as Cathy, you two should be a match."

"Hey, wait until I meet the guy first, will you? I don't want to mope around like you have since Eric flew away. Did anyone ever tell you that there are some things you can make happen, but love isn't one of them."

"Have I really been that obvious?"

"I won't answer that at this point. Back to Saturday's game. Are you planning to bring Terry?"

"Of course. Who else did you have in mind?" laughed Karyn.

"Oh, you're impossible," sighed Cindy. "I don't know how I've managed to put up with you this last year," with mock weariness in her voice.

"I'll talk to Terry when I see him at class. We could pick you up on our way to Boulder, unless you have other plans," said Karyn. The mischief in her voice clearly came through.

"Sounds great. Can't wait for the big day!" exclaimed Cindy. "Now I've gotta run."

Karyn smiled as she thought about their conversation. Cindy deserved someone special, and hopefully Mark would be that person in her life. *Hmm—Cindy married to a doctor. That would be nice, mused Karyn.*

Terry responded with enthusiasm when Karyn conveyed Cathy's invitation.

"Cathy wants us to meet at her apartment at eleven o'clock. Since it's such a mixed group, it will give us time for introductions and a snack before we go. Mark and Cindy have never met, and you haven't met any of my friends." Karyn hung up the phone, and found herself looking forward to the game and the time with friends.

A raw mid-October wind was whistling around the apartment

buildings, but the sky was clear as Terry, Karyn and Cindy made their way up the walk to Cathy's unit. Terry rang the bell, and Mark greeted them at the door. Making short work of the introductions, he took their coats and hung them in the hall closet.

"Hello, everybody," said Cathy. She came from the kitchen bringing a bucket of ice and placing it on the table in the dining area. Mark repeated the introductions when Cathy's fiance Dave walked in the front door carrying two cartons of pop and a large bag of chips.

"Well, I hate to tell you this, but the CSU Rams are going to lose today because we always win our home games," said Dave, with a confident grin.

"You know what happens if you don't? Some of our guys love to tear down the goal posts of the rival teams," said Terry, quickly responding to the light-hearted challenge. They were immediately exchanging banter about past history.

"I hate to break this up, but there are beverages, chips, and dips for a snack. Everyone help yourselves. Game time is one o'clock. We can't be late and find parking," reminded Cathy.

❖ ❖ ❖

The game was close, and the old rivalry of the two teams kept the crowd roaring.

Cindy and Mark seemed at ease when Karyn looked over to where they were seated. From all appearances, they were more interested in each other than the game. Cindy had not been seriously involved since her broken engagement, still trying to figure out what happened to her storybook romance.

At halftime, the CU Buffs were ahead by three points. Gray clouds hovered over the sky and snow began spitting into the stadium. Terry pulled out the stadium blanket they were sitting on, wrapped it around Karyn's shoulders, and pulled her close to him.

The wind whipped fine snow through the bleachers during the

fourth quarter, making spectators uncomfortable and the playing field wet and slippery. Karyn and Terry sat huddled together, holding the blanket around their shoulders, rising together to cheer CSU's scores.

True to Dave's prediction, Boulder passed the ball to Anderson for the final touchdown. CSU played hard, but didn't have the defense needed to hold the opposing team.

The spirit of rivalry and teasing continued as the group stomped the snow off their feet at Cathy's door. Throughout the evening, the football enthusiasts replayed the game.

Mark and Cindy sat in the living room oblivious to the hilarity going on in the dining room. Cathy brought in the hamburgers from the kitchen and called them for the second time to come and get their plates.

Karyn no longer needed to worry about her friend's social life if today was any indication of the couple's apparent interest in each other.

Chapter 17

Terry Has His Day

The weeks slipped by, and Karyn had heard nothing from Eric since their ski trip. She finally came to the conclusion that maybe she had been right in thinking Eric took romantic interludes none too seriously. Deliberately, clear-headed, she told herself that she understood. But that wasn't true. The truth was she felt not only disappointed in him, but hurt and angry. What started out as merely a nugget of promise in her life had grown into something more. *Maybe I sensed an intimacy that he hadn't shared. Am I always going to lose the men in my life?* Intense melancholy filled the afternoon.

Karyn began having recurring dreams about the flood, seeing people swept away before her eyes. Waking up in terror because the dreams were so real, she sat up, looking around to consciously assure herself she was safe in her own room. *Will I ever get over these horrible nightmares?* She lay back down against her pillow, only to fall into a troubled sleep.

Seeking to erase all the troubling memories from her mind, Karyn threw herself into her studies and her work. Making preparations for an open house in Wade's newest housing development, and trying to keep up her class assignments kept her busy enough to feel exhausted when she finally dropped into bed. She and Helen worked together to coordinate the color schemes for the model home. Homestead House supplied the furnishings and window coverings for the showing. Karyn loved coordinating the colors throughout the house and adding the small touches that gave the model a finished and livable appearance. It gave her special pleasure to hear potential customer's comments on her natural talent for decorating as they walked through observing the details. The busy weekend was therapeutic for the sleep-interrupted nights she had been experiencing of late. Terry had asked her out several times, but Karyn had declined his invitations. Sure that he would not understand her reasons, she had no desire to explain her complicated feelings to him. She did agree to meet him in the coffee shop to discuss one of their more difficult assignments.

"You have been avoiding me again. What did I do? I promise not to do it again if you will just tell me," he said with a mischievous grin. "Or is it this Eric that you introduced me to at Winter Park?"

Karyn assured him it was nothing he had done. Quick to change the subject, she asked him what his plans were for Thanksgiving vacation.

"You didn't answer my question, my fair lady," spoke Terry with a disarming smile and an amusing Irish brogue.

Karyn smiled into the impish brown eyes that met her own. She found Terry's sense of humor delightful and replied, "I met Eric this past summer. He's an Air Force pilot, stationed in California, and was here on leave for a few days."

"Good. I'm glad he's stationed that far away. What are your plans for Thanksgiving? Are you going home?"

"Not this year. I've got tests right after the holiday, and I need to put in some extra study time," said Karyn. Her voice conveyed a touch of disappointment. "Beside, I plan to go home for Christmas, and I can't do both."

"How about having Thanksgiving dinner with me at my apartment? That may sound like a dangerous idea on the surface, but my roommate and I decided to invite some friends in. He is a great gourmet cook, and he has promised us his very best in culinary art. We're going to do the turkey, dressing and the whole bit. I'd be most honored, my Beautiful Lady, if you would be my guest for the day." Rising from the table, Terry ceremoniously bowed from the waist and placed a kiss on the back of her hand in a style reminiscent of another era.

As other students looked on at the capers, Karyn laughed and replied, "How can I refuse an invitation like that. There is just one small request I would like to make. May I bring a cranberry salad?"

Laughing in mutual merriment, they headed in different directions for class.

Terry answered the door with a chef's apron covering his dress clothes. The aroma of sage and roasting turkey wafted throughout the apartment. Feminine laughter was interspersed with a lively conversation about the abilities of the main chef, Max. He was busily serving up the side dishes and responded, "Now, if you women don't behave, we'll leave you to do the dishes all by yourselves, and you won't get any of my fabulous dessert!"

"I think I'll stay out of trouble and light the candles on the table," said Max's girlfriend, with an impish grin. Terry took Karyn's hand, and proudly introduced her to the other six guests. It was a lively meal, full of laughter and reminiscing about past holidays.

Terry found it hard not to stare at Karyn throughout the afternoon. Already captivated by her natural charm, his heart was behaving wildly as he watched her fit so comfortably into the circle of his friends. She was obviously enjoying herself as she engaged in animated conversation with others around the dinner table. The fun continued while they all pitched in to clear the table and clean up the kitchen.

Following dinner, Terry suggested they all take an afternoon walk in the park to make up for the overindulgence of Max's cooking. Max threw the first snowball at Terry, who in turn reciprocated. A snowball fight ensued, which eventually turned into a free-for-all among the men. The women got dusted with snow in an effort to stay out of the line of fire. With rosy cheeks and wet feet, the group decided it was time to call a truce.

Lying in bed that night, Karyn thought about the events of the day. Everything they had done had been so much fun. She realized how serious her life had become over the past year. There's always something exciting going on when I'm with Terry. His outgoing personality attracts people like a magnet. Terry never left her wondering how he felt about her. It was not that he had been verbal about it, but he continued to pursue her. He was not demanding, but persistent. The thought caused her to smile as she drifted off to sleep.

❖ ❖ ❖

"We're expecting you for Christmas since you didn't make it home for Thanksgiving," Karyn's mother chided by phone. "Corrine, Randy and the twins will be here. Christmas wouldn't be complete without you."

"I wouldn't miss it for anything. In fact, I made my plane reservations before Thanksgiving. How's that for planning, Mom? School will be out the seventeenth, but I need to put in some time at work over part of the vacation. The accountant wants most of the last month's records for computing taxes. I have a Continental flight, number 715, on the twenty-fourth, arriving in Chicago at two-ten in the afternoon. By that time I'll be ready for vacation!"

Chapter 18

Emotional Conflict

Corrine and Mrs. Anderson were waiting when Karyn stepped into the terminal at the airport. The rapid exchange of information as they drove out of the airport caused them to break out in laughter. "You'd think we had just this one day to catch up," laughed Corrine.

Christmas lights blinked a welcome from the eaves of the two-story, white frame house. Two large spruce trees, flanking the front walk, cast a bright reflection on the pristine snow. Garlands of evergreen, holly, and red ribbon draped around the front door created a fragrant and welcoming archway.

Karyn's father met them at the door and gave each of his daughters a fond hug and kiss. Karyn turned to see Corrine's blond four-year-old twins standing on the sidelines, tentatively watching the adults greet each other. Karyn reached down to wrap her arms around her little niece and nephew, planting a kiss on each of their cheeks. She asked, "How are my two little sweethearts?" Taking their hands she turned to survey the room.

"Mother, the house is so beautiful and festive! It's so good to be home. I'd hate to miss Christmas with the family," she said, releasing the twins and giving her mother an affectionate hug.

"Come into the kitchen while I put the final touches on dinner," said Mrs. Anderson, hurrying to check the ham in the oven.

"No wonder we all love holidays," said Randy as he seated Corrine. He perused the well-laden dinner table and said, "Makes me hungry just to look at it."

The entire family gathered around the dinner table, and Karyn's mother and father had never looked happier as they smiled at each other. At that moment, Karyn wanted nothing more than to be able to duplicate the love and trust shinning from her parents eyes.

Linking hands around the table, the family bowed their heads as Mr. Anderson prayed, "Thank you, Father, for each family member gathered here on this special holiday. How privileged we are to be the recipients of all your gracious provisions this past year. As we celebrate the Savior's birth, may we truly be mindful of the price He paid for our sin. For it's in His name we pray. Amen."

The evergreen centerpiece gave off an aroma of pine as the flame from the large red candle flickered in the center of the table, spread with a holiday feast. The ham, spiked with whole cloves, scalloped potatoes, broccoli and cauliflower in cheese sauce, cranberry salad, dinner rolls, and condiments crowded the table. A huge tray of holiday cookies and her grandmother's crystal punch bowl, filled with sparkling punch, stood on the sideboard.

The warmth of her family's presence surrounded Karyn as she looked around the dinner table. She realized at that moment how much she had missed each of them, and how good it was to be home at this special season of the year.

After dinner, her father lit the fireplace while the women finished cleaning up the kitchen. The twins, dressed in their red

Christmas pajamas, came to encourage the ladies to hurry up. "Grandpa's going to read the Christmas story to us before we have to go to bed."

Mr. Anderson sat in his favorite recliner with the reading lamp close at hand and his Bible opened in front of him. Corrine dimmed the other lights to fully enjoy the beauty of the multicolored lights on the Christmas tree. The twins sat on the floor in front of the tree, gazing at the enormous number of brightly wrapped packages beneath the ornament-laden evergreen boughs.

The wonder of the nativity account gripped Karyn anew as she listened intently to the sound of her dad's voice reading the familiar passage, which he had done every Christmas she could remember.

Later, from the upstairs hallway, Karyn heard the routine sounds of family—her dad and mom talking as they shut off the lights, Corrine saying bedtime prayer with the twins, and Randy on the phone wishing his parents a Merry Christmas.

In her bedroom, Karyn glanced around the room with a sense of nostalgia at the sight of her high school annuals stacked in the bookcase, the snapshot of her posing in her cheerleading uniform tucked in the mirror, and her favorite doll in a small rocking chair. It was like stepping back into her teen years.

As the house grew silent, and the rest of the family retired for the night, Corrine slipped into Karyn's room. In their bathrobes, the two sisters sat curled up on the bed. It seemed like the years had never passed since they had done the same thing when they were growing up.

"So who's the current man in your life since I haven't heard much about your pilot friend lately?"

Karyn related the events of the past few months while she had been dating Terry. "He is so much fun to be with, but I'm still not sure how serious I am about him. I just can't seem to get Eric out of my mind. Silly, when I haven't heard from him in over a month," said Karyn, drawing finger patterns in the bedspread.

"You really have a crush on the guy, don't you?"

There was a wistful expression on Karyn's face as she answered the question she found difficult to express verbally.

"I'll never forget my first date with Randy," said Corrine, a far away look in her eyes. "He was my one and only serious relationship. My roommate at college talked me into going on a blind date with a friend of her boyfriend. It's hard to believe, but Randy told me on the first date he was going to marry me," laughed Corrine. "A man true to his word."

❖ ❖ ❖

Randy and Corrine left before New Years Day so he could get back to his dental practice.

Karyn cherished the time alone with her parents. She sensed her mother was worried about her. Her father looked uncertain when he brought up the subject of Eric, "her pilot friend."

She could tell they wanted to ask questions about him, but were reluctant to do so because Karyn had barely mentioned him, while earlier his name had been prominent in every letter. They were puzzled by Karyn's silence, and yet could read the hurt in her eyes when they asked about him.

Without further prying, her dad quietly said to her, "Just leave everything in God's hands. If it's real love, examining it won't hurt it or change it."

❖ ❖ ❖

Christmas at home had surpassed all of Karyn's expectations. While the holidays had come and gone, Karyn had heard nothing from Eric.

The following Thursday after class, Terry caught up with Karyn to ask, "What are you doing this weekend? The weather is perfect for skiing. Why don't you and I go for the weekend?"

Karyn looked thoughtful for a moment and replied, "I'd love to."

"We could ski on Saturday, and take one of those dinner sleigh rides on Sunday," said Terry, with boyish enthusiasm. "Have you ever done that?"

"No, but it sounds like great fun. Give me a call when you work out the details. Right now, I need to finish some reports at the office."

The weekend with Terry proved to be all that he had promised. They skied on Saturday until they were exhausted. That night they went out for dinner, and then came back to Karyn's room at Summit House to make popcorn. Sitting in front of a blazing fire in the fireplace, they watched Rock Hudson and Doris Day in a TV comedy, "Send Me No Flowers."

Following the late movie, the dancing firelight from the fireplace sent shifting highlights over their faces. Terry was like a playful friend until time to say good night, and then he became quietly serious.

Gently pulling Karyn into his arms, he kissed her good night. She yielded to his embrace, and tentatively returned his gentle kiss, as if to test their relationship. Terry's second kiss was firm and more persuasive, seeking a response. Releasing her, Terry said good night and started to walk to the door, not trusting himself to say more. At the door he turned with a mischievous grin, "You know, we could save the price of a room if you'd invite me to stay."

"Sorry, but my mother raised old fashioned girls." Smiling, Karyn gave him a playful push out the door. "See you in the morning."

It's getting harder and harder to resist Terry. I feel like I'm on an emotional roller-coaster.

Karyn stood before the bathroom mirror, pulling her hair back into a barrette, when the phone rang.

"Hey, Beautiful, are you ready for a sleigh ride today?"

"I can't wait! Sounds wonderful."

"I'll meet you in the lounge in ten minutes for some breakfast. I'm starved." Terry looked at his watch, wanting to make the most of every moment of the day.

When they started for the dining room, a young woman in ski apparel turned into Karyn without realizing Karyn's nearness behind her.

"Oh, I'm sorry...Karyn! I haven't seen you for ages. I kept meaning to call you after I heard about Jim's death, but just got busy and never did. You know how that is. It must have been terrible for you." Looking at Terry apologetically, she realized from the puzzled look on his face, that he was clearly in the dark about the conversation.

"Yes, it's still hard to believe. Jennifer, I want you to meet a friend of mine, Terry Hughs."

"It's nice to meet you, Terry. Sorry for going on and on, but it's been some time since I've seen Karyn. She and I used to live in the same apartment complex. It's so good to see you, Karyn. Give me a call. We need to get together for lunch. I'd better hurry or my party will be leaving without me."

"What was that all about?" Terry gave Karyn a questioning look.

The question left her searching for a reply. Karyn shook her head, trying to dismiss the subject she was so reluctant to discuss.

When they were seated with their coffee, Terry looked across the table at her, waiting for an answer to his question. Always hesitant to press her in the past, he refused to ignore the obviously painful subject. "You've never told me what that was all about."

"I know. I suppose it's something I'd like to bury as if it never happened. Maybe it's guilt on my part, but it's hardly the kind of thing you want to tell your friends. Jim drowned in the Big Thompson flood."

"Karyn, why should you feel guilty about that?" asked Terry, with a mystified expression on his face.

"We were good friends, and I left him to move his car while I fled up the mountain. I will always wonder if I did the right thing." Tears welled up in Karyn's eyes, and she felt her throat constrict.

"Why didn't he go with you?"

"He had a brand new Porsche, and he thought he had time to move it closer to the canyon wall to protect it. He told me to climb to safety, and he would follow me up. Jim drowned trying to save the car."

"Oh, Karyn. I'm sorry." Taking both of her hands across the table in a sympathetic gesture, his eyes softened as he looked at her and saw the visible pain in her face.

The waitress brought their order of pancakes and sausage, interrupting their strained conversation.

Terry wanted to take Karyn in his arms to comfort her. "I can't imagine the kind of man who would be responsible for leaving you with that load of guilt. It seems like he should have been more concerned about your safety instead of his car. Karyn, I think you have a massive case of survivor guilt.

"I'm glad you finally told me what happened. I hoped the time would come when you felt like sharing whatever it was in the past that troubled you." His face lit up with the most teasing smile and, winking across the table, he said, "I was beginning to think all kinds of things. Like maybe you were married, and you were afraid to tell me."

The irony of it couldn't help but bring a smile to Karyn's face.

Chapter 19

Eric's Plane Goes Down

The Cold War in Europe continued between Communist nations trying to spread their ideology, and democratic nations determined to contain the spread of Communism. Concerned about a military build-up, the United States was vigilant in maintaining surveillance over Russia in case of a military build-up.

The euphoria Eric experienced when he settled behind the control panel of the SR-71 was a pilot's dream, matched only by his Reconnaissance System Officer in the rear seat. The training had been as vigorous as that demanded from astronauts, but he and Rod had survived the intense selection process.

Now Eric looked back on the three years of flying at altitudes and speed once thought impossible.

The "Blackbird," capable of flying 2,070 miles an hour, astounded the experts because it was extremely advanced for its time. Built for strategic reconnaissance, the plane was shrouded in secrecy. Shaped like a glider, its payload consisted of camera equipment capable of surveying 100,000 square miles per hour, and flying above the range of anti-aircraft fire.

Eric's jet flew as low as his orders permitted while the cameras continued to photograph suspicious ground installations in Russia. They were nearly ready to complete their mission and return to a neutral zone when suddenly the forward fuselage tank indicated a high rate of fuel leakage. The plane began pitching out of control. An explosion jarred the forward fuselage area.

Breaking radio silence, Rod shouted, "We've got a fire aboard."

"Rod, bail out! The alarm system says eject!"

Reacting instantly and instinctively, Eric shouted into his radio, "975 declaring an emergency, 975 declaring an emergency." With five fuel tanks in the fuselage, he had no choice but to reach for the ejection seat handle located between his legs. When he gave a sharp tug upward, the canopy unlocked, and he was thrust from the aircraft. Much to his dismay, one of the cables locking his left leg in the seating position came loose, allowing his leg to flail in the air. A crushing pain went through his whole body. He nearly blacked out. Aware his pressure suit had opened immediately, he breathed in the oxygen. *I can't pass out...have to pull...the release handle...on the survival kit!* The drogue chute, attached to the top of the ejection seat, kept him from tumbling during the long "free fall". *Can't pass out...pull release handle...survival kit...or life raft...won't open.* He passed out.

❖ ❖ ❖

Eric's plane went down in a burst of flame over the Baltic Sea. Barely conscious in the frigid water, it was all he could do to keep his head above water. He managed to hang on to his life raft, but he didn't have the strength to pull himself up and get his broken leg over the side. It was useless in the water. The cold helped to numb the pain, but the struggle to keep from passing out made survival seem impossible. He could see something in the blurring distance, but didn't have the strength to call out for help. *Is it part of the plane or something else?* His eyes slid shut as the pain enveloped his body. He slipped into a black hole, which began to close in upon him. Eric came out of a foggy semiconscious state as two men hauled him aboard a small fishing boat. He knew he should be frightened, but he couldn't feel anything anymore.

❖ ❖ ❖

The SR Command knew Eric's plane had gone down, but had no further communication from either pilot. Since the government would have to deny they were responsible for having a surveillance plane in Russian air space, nothing was reported concerning the missing plane.

Karyn's unopened letters were placed among Eric's personal belongings.

Chapter 20

A Letter Arrives

The holidays had come and gone, and Karyn had heard nothing from Eric. Each day she went to her mailbox, secretly hoping for a letter in his handwriting. She tried not to be too disappointed when there was none. However, today to Karyn's astonishment, an overseas letter in a stilted script, with a foreign stamp and postmark lay among the other pieces of mail. When Karyn opened the envelope, the letter was signed by a nurse at the U.S. Air Force Hospital in Bitburg, Germany.

A shock like an electrical current went through Karyn. She couldn't believe what she was reading!

"Eric was injured in a plane crash during a military mission on January 21, 1977. He was picked up by a fishing vessel following the crash and is recovering in our U.S. hospital in Bitburg."

The letter continued. "Eric was able to eject from the burning plane, but sustained serious physical injuries, as well as hypothermia from being in the cold water until he was rescued. We've managed to stabilize his condition, but he is not yet able to personally contact you. It is uncertain at this time how long he might need to remain in Germany. He was very concerned that

140

you know what had happened."

Karyn immediately sat down to write to Eric.

Dearest Eric,

You can't imagine how shocked I was to hear about your plane crash. The nurse didn't say anything regarding the nature of your injuries, but she did indicate you were lucky to be alive. It's hard to think about you recovering so far away and not to know your day-to-day progress.

Since it has been several months since I've heard from you, I've had visions of some beautiful gal stealing you away, and I would never see or hear from you again. I envy the nurses who are there to take care of you.

Is there anything I can send you to make your hospital stay more comfortable?

My Love,

Karyn

All the former apprehension was gone. Karyn no longer gave any consideration to the fact she might be taking too much for granted. Although Eric had never expressed his true feelings about their future, he cared enough to contact her as soon as he could. Her spirit soared.

To be in love was such a glorious feeling, an exhilaration that transcended anything she had previously known. Her only concern now, how serious were his injuries? How soon would he be returning to the States?

She thought about the first day she had seen Eric on the rafting trip and again when he piloted the rescue aircraft. What chemistry singled out this one person in the midst of all the chaos, and every other face became a blur? *Love pays little heed to logic. But I would have to have been blind not to notice how attractive he was. Is it his rugged handsomeness, or his gentle, caring concern that makes him so appealing?* Never before had she felt someone had become the very center of her life.

Lying in a hospital bed in Germany, Eric was coping with his own personal dilemmas. He awoke with a terrible, twisting pain gripping his body from the internal injuries he had suffered. When his vision cleared, he looked down to see his leg in a cast and elevated at the foot of his bed. Fortunately, he had escaped serious burns because the plane sustained damage in the rear. Then fear hit him like a punch in the midsection. Sucking in his breath, he thought, *What happened to Rod? What if we can never fly again?*

A man with salt-and-pepper gray hair, dressed in a white coat, appeared at Eric's bedside. "I'm Doctor James. I'm glad you've decided to return to the land of the living. It's been touch and go. I have to say you are a very lucky young man. We thought for a time we might lose you."

"Doc, what happened to the other pilot?" Eric held his breath waiting for the reply, fear registered in his eyes.

"Your friend is fine. He was released two days ago. His pressure suit probably saved his life. He could have been severely burned."

"For the first time in my life, I think there just might be a God who looks down and rescues guys like me," Eric said, wincing with pain.

"I'm glad to see you're awake and feeling something. I'll have a nurse come in and give you a shot to relieve the pain."

A nurse stepped in to assist the doctor and administered the prescribed medication. Soon Eric drifted into a state where reality became a fuzzy blur. Succumbing to the sedative, he mumbled, "Gotta fly again."

Hearing muffled voices, Eric opened his eyes and saw several doctors and his nurse standing at his bedside in consultation.

"Well, Doc, are you going to be able to patch me up so I can fly again?"

"Right now the nurse is going to change your dressings, and we're going to take a look to see how you're healing following surgery. When you're feeling a little better, we'll take you down to X-ray to check on that leg."

The doctor refused to assure him he would completely recover from his injuries. His standard reply was, "It's too soon to tell. You're lucky to be alive. Let's just take one thing at a time."

"When we finish with your dressings," said the nurse, "you have some company here to see you. Your parents flew in today."

"My parents!" Eric looked up to see his mother peeking in the door and his father standing in the hall behind her.

The nurse gathered the soiled dressings and tossed them into a sanitary disposal. Walking to the door she said, "You may come in now. I'm sure your son is anxious to see you."

Mrs. Johnson took a quick look at Eric's pale face and at the leg elevated above the foot of the bed. She walked to the bedside and leaned down to kiss Eric on the forehead. "Your dad and I have been so worried about you. We had to come."

"Son, we got a telegram about your accident, but they didn't give us any details." Eric's dad reached out to grasp Eric's hand in both of his. How did it happen?"

Father and son discussed the details of the plane's malfunction and the crash that followed. Mrs. Johnson just shook her head, realizing how close her son had come to instant death. She looked around the room and checked the items on the bedside table. "Is there anything we can bring you? Do you have something to read?"

"You could bring me some books. Since I have to lie on my back until they take my leg out of this sling, that's about all I can do."

Eric smiled at his parents, pleased they had come. "How long do you plan to stay?"

"We'll stick around most of this week to make sure these doctors and nurses treat you right," said his dad with a twinkle in his eye.

"The nurse said we shouldn't stay too long," said Mrs. Johnson as she looked solicitously at her eldest son. "Matt sends his love. He would like to have come too, but he just started a new job and didn't feel he could leave."

"Now, Mom and Dad, I want you to see some of the attractions in this country while you're here. I don't want you to think you have to sit by my bedside all the time. Do you hear?"

❖ ❖ ❖

Eric's parents stopped by the hospital each morning and evening to check on his progress.

"I finally got out of bed today," said Eric. "Since the swelling has gone down, the doctor had them remove the sling. One of the nurses wheeled me down to the lab for an X-ray. The doctor isn't real pleased the way the leg is healing. It may require some more surgery."

"Oh, son, we hope not." Mrs. Johnson's face wore an anxious expression. "We have to leave tomorrow."

"Mom, don't worry. I have the finest doctors the military has available."

❖ ❖ ❖

While Eric recuperated, he had time to contemplate the loss of his plane. It seemed almost like a personal tragedy. The period of intense training for surveillance had created a magical fascination for the abilities of the SR-71. His amazing aircraft was destroyed in a few seconds off the coast of Russia.

As Eric thought about the accident, he was reminded of how fragile the thread of life could be. Karyn was constantly on his mind.

Her letter arrived! Eric hastily tore it open. Mental pictures flooded his memory as he read the words. Her delicate features, dark hair curving around her oval face, dark brows, naturally arched, and thickly fringed lashes were stamped on his brain. There was a spiritual kind of beauty about her. She had a gentle and quiet spirit within. He could still remember how it felt to hold her in his arms. He knew his feelings had not been a passing whim. *What if I had died in the crash and could never see her again?* The very thought gave him a sense of urgency to get well and get back to the States.

Once during the time he was recuperating, Eric awoke to find his nurse hovering over him. For a moment he thought it was Karyn. But no...the eyes were the wrong color.

❖ ❖ ❖

Two weeks after the accident, he called Karyn.

The timbre of his voice on the overseas line sent a flood of sensations pulsing throughout Karyn's body. How long she had waited to hear his voice! The phone call stirred up all the poignant memories of the times they had been together.

"You asked me if there was something you could send me, and there is one thing. I don't have a picture of you to show off to these guys in the hospital ward."

"I think I can manage that without too much difficulty," she said, with a smile. "Besides, I don't want those flirty nurses to think you have no ties back home. Judging from the request, you must be feeling better."

❖ ❖ ❖

Eric's calls became more frequent as his injuries continued to heal. Following his calls, Karyn felt a sense of restlessness that she couldn't explain. *What would happen if I just dropped everything and flew to Germany? Could I really just leave all my responsibilities to do something so impulsive? My head has always ruled my heart in the past. Since Eric has come into my world, all common sense seems to have fled. Lord, what can happen to save me from this insanity?*

Eric called!

"I think they are going to ship me home in a few weeks if the doctor agrees I'm mending well enough to be released," Eric said, trying to keep his voice calm, even though he felt like shouting. Missing her had become almost like a physical pain. "I'm planning to spend my medical leave in Fort Collins if the Air Force gives me clearance. Think you can put up with this fly-boy for a few weeks? I plan to monopolize as much of your time as you let me. Okay? I've missed you, Karyn, and I've had a lot of time to think about us while I've been in the hospital."

"I've missed you, too. It's been hard to have you so far away and not to be able to get a daily report on your progress."

"I'll tell you all about it when I get home. My doctor is here. I have to go. I'll call you when they tell me how soon I'm getting out of here."

Karyn hung up the phone and stared off into space. Her face glowed with a soft, dreamy expression. Even after Eric hung up, the conversation continued to replay in her mind for minutes to follow. Questions began to plague her. *Do I really know the extent of Eric's injuries? Will his male pride allow him to tell me? Will he be able to fly again? Will I always be wondering where he is and how long before he can contact me again? How do we resolve the problems of time and distance? Do I want that kind of life for myself?*

Karyn went to her stereo and put on a record. Sitting down with a cup of tea, she looked around her comfortable condo. She thought back to the day she had signed the contract with the realtor. She had made a sizeable down payment with an inheritance her grandmother had left her. The floral-on-white sofa and love seat, tossed with pillows of turquoise and avocado, the brass and glass coffee and end tables she had recently purchased with one of her bonus checks, gave her a sense of pleasure. *I have just reached a comfortable plateau of work and school that make my life seem secure and predictable. Can I give that up for the uncertainty a life with Eric might involve?*

The romantic melody in the background reminded her of the last night Eric had been in her apartment, and they had danced around the living room. There had been no fear of the future then. At that moment, she would have gone anywhere with him! Questions crowded her mind. *Why the sudden doubts now? Is it because I fear he might be disabled? If I let him get away, will I regret it for the rest of my life? Would love mean always being a little afraid?*

How will I explain my feelings to Terry? How do I tell him that Eric is the main focus of my life?

Shaking her head in frustration at the confusion of her emotions, Karyn reached for the phone to call Cindy. "How about lunch and shopping on this gorgeous Saturday?"

"I'd love to. Where shall we go?"

"Let's go to Denver and see what's new in the malls. I haven't been shopping there for ages," Karyn said, as she glanced at the anniversary clock on her mantle.

"Sounds good to me. There's something I need to talk to you about, and I've been meaning to call you. The drive will give us plenty of time to visit."

Karyn could sense something was terribly wrong the minute she saw Cindy. She looked tired with dark circles under her eyes, and she seemed extremely nervous, which was out of character for her.

"I'm glad you're driving. I didn't sleep well last night, and I would hate the thought of navigating traffic this morning. In fact, I haven't had a good night's sleep in two weeks," Cindy said, lowering the passenger seat into a reclining position.

"What's going on, Cindy?"

"For the past two weeks I've been getting these late night phone calls every couple of hours. No one says anything. Whoever it is just breathes into the phone until I hang up. Finally, I decided not to answer the phone, but it just keeps ringing. I talked to the phone company about it, and they installed a temporary box on the phone to find out where the calls are coming from.

Apparently, whoever is doing it is using different pay phones in the area so they can't be traced."

"Why didn't you call and come stay with me? I wouldn't stay there another night!" exclaimed Karyn.

"When I talked to the police, they said they would send a patrol car around in the area periodically. They might be able to catch the guy phoning or prowling around the neighborhood."

"You said 'guy'?"

"I'm sure it is a man. The policeman said that's not the type of thing women normally do. If I leave they might not find out who it is. I seem to be the only one the police have talked to who is getting these calls. They suspect it's someone that I know, or a man who lives in our apartment complex. A very comforting thought!"

"How can you stand to stay there under those circumstances? What if the guy is really dangerous?"

"They don't think I'm in any danger. He seems to be just a crank caller looking for some excitement in his life. Paula, from the office, has offered to come and stay with me this next week. I'm so glad you suggested this trip. The whole thing has really started to get on my nerves."

Chapter 21

Time to Remember

K aryn slipped into a white linen suit, tucked a red and white polka-dot scarf into the neck of the jacket, and stepped back to examine her image in the mirror. Satisfied, she picked up her purse, and checked the flight arrival schedule for the fourth time.

Eric was due in at three forty-five on Continental. Her mind raced. *How will it be to see him after months of separation? Will it be the same as I've imagined each time I've thought of him? Are my expectations of this meeting too lofty? Will I be disappointed?* Karyn realized all the mental gymnastics in the world were not going to prepare her for this moment. She had to take whatever risk the future held for the two of them.

She paced nervously at the window of Stapleton Airport, watching while a Continental plane pulled up to the concourse. Travelers poured out from the departure door, and she caught a glimpse of Eric behind the other passengers. Her heart skipped a beat when he started toward her. In dress uniform, tie crisply knotted, and the visor of his hat pulled to a proper horizontal level, he was visibly limping and using a cane. An attractive stewardess followed him, carrying his flight bags.

When Karyn rushed up to meet him, her eyes were shining and a smile of pleasure softened her lips.

Eric dropped his cane and threw his arms around her. He kissed her soundly, oblivious to the stewardess standing there with an envious look on her face. Feelings so strong and poignant overwhelmed Karyn. Eric had reached into her soul and brought out emotions she hadn't known she could feel.

"If you will wait a minute, I'll call a porter to take your bags for you," said the stewardess, as Eric released Karyn. Smiling, he said, "That would be fine, and thanks for your help."

The porter arrived on a baggage car, and Karyn and Eric stepped on. She saw that it took all of Eric's reserve of strength to walk just a short distance. Rather than embarrass him, Karyn said to the porter, "Could you please take us to our car?"

"Normally, we don't do that, but this time I guess I could make an exception," he said with an expression of sympathy on his face.

Eric gave Karyn a grateful look. "I guess I'm not as ready to assume civilian life as I thought."

Once settled in the car, Eric turned to Karyn, "You don't know how I've counted the days until I'd get home to see you. I have two weeks of medical leave before I have to check into Fitzsimmons Hospital for a routine checkup. I hope you have me on your calendar every day for the next two weeks." He studied her face, the image that had often kept him awake at night in the hospital, between lights out and sleep.

Karyn laughed. "You know I'm a working girl, but I plan to take some time off. Where to, Captain?"

"I have reservations at the Holiday Inn. I'll get checked in, and then we'll plan our two weeks. Okay?"

During the hour-and-a-half drive from Denver to Fort Collins, Karyn listened quietly while Eric related guarded details of his overseas accident and the time he spent in Germany convalescing. She felt a knot in her stomach, realizing how close to death he had come.

Eric sighed, "If it hadn't been for those fishermen who witnessed the mid-air explosion and rescued me, I'd never have made it in those frigid waters. When they pulled me onto the boat, I didn't know if they were friend or foe.

My doctor was still reluctant to release me from the hospital, but I gave them such fits about going home, they were glad to get rid of me, and put me on a plane for Denver."

Karyn let Eric out at the door of the Holiday Inn. He walked stiffly to the entrance while she pulled around to park the car. Eric stood waiting in the lobby for her, while a porter went to the car for the luggage. When Karyn walked in, Eric guided her toward the dining room. "Let's have some lunch, and then I need to get out of this uniform."

Following lunch, Karyn said, "This has been a hard day for you. I'm going to run home to take care of some things, while you get some rest this afternoon. How about dinner at my place this evening?"

"You mean you can cook, too? How could I be fortunate enough to find all these qualities in one woman?" The tone was light, but the look in Eric's eyes said a great deal more as he walked her to the door.

"Dinner will be ready at six-thirty. Shall I pick you up about six o'clock?"

Eric acknowledged with a nod and a smile.

❖ ❖ ❖

Karyn stepped out her door to cut a bouquet of pink and white peonies blooming beside her doorstep. She breathed in the fragrance as she carried them into the condo and placed them in a vase on the dinner table. Then she checked the chicken in the oven. Satisfied that dinner would soon be ready, she picked up her car keys to go to the Holiday to get Eric.

"This looks like dining at the Ritz with candles and the works. Is the maitre d' serving us, too?" laughed Eric, as he seated Karyn. Eric pushed away from the table following a dinner of chicken-cordon-bleu, parsleyed potatoes, and spinach salad, topped off with strawberry shortcake for dessert. "Where did you learn to cook like that?" he asked.

"I liked helping my mother in the kitchen. We had many wonderful times planning meals for guests on special occasions."

As Karyn started clearing away the dishes, she asked, "How would you like to drive up Poudre Canyon? It's such a beautiful evening. Do you feel up to it?"

"Sounds great to me. What happened up Poudre Canyon during the flood? I never did hear anything on the news."

"Fortunately it sustained very little damage."

"Let's go. Later this week, I'd like to drive up Big Thompson Canyon to see what it looks like after the flood. Have you been back since last summer?"

"No. I couldn't bear to go back because of all the tragedy I remember there. Now I think I might be up to it."

Karyn leisurely drove through Fort Collins, detouring from the main route to show Eric some of the attractions of the city. They drove down College Avenue, around the library, and back past City Park to Laurel Street.

"This is CSU's campus where I've been spending a lot of my time during the last few years," said Karyn, with a reflective smile.

She drove through the center of the campus and around the historic oval drive, with its sentinels of tall elm trees creating an arch of shimmering green. The sunlight filtered through the rippling leaves, casting lacy shadows on the sidewalk below. Circling the campus to point out the various buildings, Karyn exited the campus going west on Elizabeth Street. The area was a hub of activity for students shopping or looking for short-order meals.

"What's the big dam off to the west?" asked Eric, as they drove south on Overland Trail. "And what does the big A on the hillside stand for?"

"Originally Colorado State was an agricultural college, Colorado A & M, until they made it a state university. Each year the freshmen get to paint the A as part of their initiation rites. The dam you see is Horsetooth Reservoir, named after the rock formation on the mountain top west of it."

Driving up a graveled road to the dam, they parked on a cliff overlooking the seven-mile reservoir. From there they could see the marina dock and boats skimming the lake as they pulled water skiers in the wake. The mountains, blue-hued and hazy in the late afternoon sun, formed a backdrop off to the west. At the northern dam of the lake, rolling green pastures met pine-robed foothills at the base of the mountains.

Overland Trail, a street name after the famous stage line, took them through the small town of Laporte, past Verns Café, and to Ted's Place.

Karyn loved the scenic drive along the course of the winding Poudre River. Tall pines and myriad wild flowers graced the rocky hillsides.

"Look at all the kayakers going down the river! At the first turnout, let's stop and watch them." Karyn smiled at Eric's enthusiasm as they observed the kayaks bouncing along the swiftly moving current, occasionally swirling cross-current until they could again paddle with the flow. A stranded kayaker stood on the opposite bank as some fellow enthusiasts struggled to recover his floating craft.

"Is there a good place for us to get out and walk a little? After sitting thirteen hours on the plane, this leg is giving me fits."

Approaching Diamond Rock picnic area, Karyn pulled off at the side of the road to park. They stood at the roadside looking down at the river.

Eric reached for Karyn's hand. "Shall we go down by the water? After spending so much time in California cities, I am fascinated by the Colorado mountains. I want to get a closer look at the river. Remember how much fun it was to go rafting last summer? We'll have to do that again."

Waiting for Eric to grab the handrail to go down the steps, Karyn paused and breathed deeply. "I love the smell of the pines on a warm day."

Across the river Karyn saw two deer, heads raised in alertness, staring at them from the hillside. Karyn quietly pointed them out to Eric. They stood fascinated as the deer fed, making their way slowly up the slope to move out of sight.

Standing by the river, Eric pulled Karyn close to him as they listened to the sound of the water cascading over the rocks. There was so much to say, so much to feel, and so little time for the two of them.

Breaking the silence, Eric turned to face her. "There were some times when I thought I might never see you again. That was my biggest disappointment as I floated around in the water before the fishermen picked me up. I had to get back to the States to tell you I love you, Karyn."

Karyn lifted her face to the gathering twilight, breathing in the fragrant scent of pines and savoring the stillness of the evening. When she turned her head, she met Eric's eyes, and he was already bending over to kiss her.

The last remaining glow of a gold-orange afternoon sun sank behind the mountains, and the cool night air brushed their faces. Karyn stood cuddled in the warmth of Eric's arms and felt a security she had never before known.

❖ ❖ ❖

After Karyn said good night to Eric at the Holiday Inn, it suddenly occurred to her that she had not talked to Cindy in several days. It was late, but she knew it was important to check on her friend when she got home.

"Cindy, I'm sorry to be calling you so late, but I just couldn't go to bed without knowing if the police have been able to trace the man who has been calling you? I've been so worried about you. I've been praying for your safety and trusting the police would soon catch this creep."

"I should have called you, but I knew Eric was coming in today. Yes, they found the man. It turned out to be someone on the maintenance staff here, and he used one of the office phones last night. They traced the call, and since it was after hours, no one else was in the office. He was on probation from another offense, so I don't expect he'll be bothering me again.

"Now on to happier things," said Cindy. "When do I get to see Mr. Fantastic?"

"You won't be hurt if you don't get to see Eric this time will you? He really needs his rest and time to get his strength back. His accident was more serious than he led me to believe."

"I understand. Besides, you two need time to get reacquainted. Keep me posted on how this relationship progresses."

Karyn hung up the phone, and sighed with relief. Cindy was her best friend, and Karyn felt a stab of guilt thinking about her own happiness. How reluctant she was to let anything spoil the elation she felt. *With Eric here it's just hard to keep both feet on the ground. Lord, forgive me for being so selfish when my dearest friend has been going through such a difficult time.*

The next few days passed quickly as Karyn worked in the mornings and took the afternoons off to spend with Eric. Each day she could see him improve as he relaxed and rested during the week. They spent lazy afternoons swimming in the pool at City Park and basking in the sun until they could tolerate the heat no longer.

"Let's go to Estes Park tomorrow," Eric said, as he rolled from his stomach to turn his tanned body toward Karyn. "I feel like tackling an out-of-town trip. What do you say?"

She sat up, her lithe figure outlined in a Hawaiian print swimsuit. A thoughtful expression crossed her face. "I'm glad you suggested it. It will be easier since we're going together."

"Are you sure? I wouldn't want anything to spoil our day."

Consciously ignoring the little twinge of anxiety she felt, Karyn smiled and said, "I'll pack us a picnic, and we'll have lunch along the way."

"Sounds good. I don't know about you, but I'm beginning feel slightly fried," said Eric. "Shall we take one more dip in the pool, pack up, and get out of the sun?"

"Right now, I could use a cold glass of lemonade. How about you? First, I'll race you to the end of the pool and back," said Karyn, as she quickly dove into the water.

Laughing, Eric followed her lead.

When they reached the shallow water and stood up, Eric quipped, "You cheat, but since you're such a pretty mermaid, I'll forgive you."

"Let's go to the condo and make a salad or something for dinner. This evening there's a concert in the park if you'd like to go," said Karyn. She picked up her suntan lotion, folded the beach towels, and stuffed them into her tote bag.

"If we're going to a concert, I'll need to go back to the Holiday and shower first," said Eric. "I just brought shorts and a T-shirt to change into."

"That's no problem. It's casual. While I make the salad, you can shower if you like," suggested Karyn.

❖ ❖ ❖

As Karyn started taking the ingredients for a taco salad out of the refrigerator, she said, "You'll find clean towels in the bathroom linen closet."

Karyn was setting the table out on the lanai when she heard a motorcycle in front of the condo. Going to the kitchen, she saw

Terry sliding off his machine. Karyn hesitated, wondering what to say to him. She walked to the door to greet him.

"It's a perfect evening for a motorcycle ride up the canyon. How about it?" Terry called out as he walked up the steps to the door.

"I'm sorry, Terry, but I have company."

"Probably should have called first, but the idea just struck me as I was pulling out of the garage."

Just then, Eric walked out of the bathroom, carrying his wet towel and swimsuit over his arm. "Karyn, what shall I do...?" and seeing Terry at the door, he paused in embarrassment.

Terry's face registered open amazement when he saw Eric. He stood glowering at Eric for several speechless seconds.

What Karyn saw written on Terry's face clearly told her what he was thinking.

"Terry, you remember Eric?" asked Karyn, a hint of anxiousness in her eyes. "Eric is on a two-week furlough. We just got back from swimming, and I was making a salad for dinner. Would you like to join us?"

"No, but thanks anyway. Think I'll just wander up the road," he said, turning to walk down the stairs and back to his bike.

Karyn stood rooted to the spot while Terry started the Harley and roared out of the parking lot. She released the breath she hadn't been aware she'd been holding.

"Sorry for the lousy timing," said Eric, as he studied Karyn's face. "That was rather an awkward position for the guy to be in."

"I don't think I've ever seen Terry when he was so totally at a loss for words," reflected Karyn.

"Maybe I should have gone back to the Holiday to clean up. I wouldn't want to cause any embarrassment for you," said Eric, a concerned expression on his face.

"Don't worry about it. At some point, I may have an opportunity to explain that things weren't as it might seem," said Karyn, as she poured iced lemonade into frosty glasses.

Following the evening concert, Karyn drove Eric to the Holiday Inn. Before getting out, he turned to Karyn. "I can't tell you how much it has meant to me to have this time with you." He pulled Karyn into his arms to kiss her.

She didn't even try to fight the emotion surging through her. She loved him!

Holding her close, Eric gazed into her eyes and pushed the dark hair away from her face with his fingers. "While I'm away I'll be able to remember you in the places that are familiar to you. Every detail is important…to be stored away and remembered while I'm gone."

❖ ❖ ❖

When Karyn started to climb into bed, she remembered the look on Terry's face when he saw Eric coming out of the bathroom. She looked at the clock on the bedside table thinking, I should call Terry. Knowing him, he is probably still up.

Terry answered the phone immediately, and Karyn could hear the murmur of the television in the background.

"I'm sorry to be calling you so late, Terry, but I felt you needed an explanation for this afternoon."

"You don't owe me an explanation. You're free to do whatever you please. I was just surprised Eric seemed to have special privileges while you have continued to keep me at arm's length. He seemed to be making himself quite at home!"

Karyn could hear the anger and sarcasm in Terry's voice. "Terry, Eric has his own room at the Holiday Inn. I merely suggested he shower here rather than going back to the motel to clean up. It wasn't what it might have looked like to you."

"As I said before, you can do what you please. I am just a little surprised that the things I admired about you have suddenly appeared to have changed."

"That's why I wanted to call you and explain a rather awkward situation for all of us. I could tell by the look on your face what you were thinking. We have been good friends, Terry, and I wouldn't want you to think badly of me."

"Yeah, we're good friends, all right. Karyn, you've meant a great deal more than that to me."

The earnestness in Terry's voice sent a wave of sadness through Karyn.

"I know you haven't felt the same about me, but I kept hoping that might change," continued Terry. "I guess after today, I realize that it will never happen. It's just as well I know it now."

"I'm sorry, Terry. You've been a wonderful friend, and we've had great times together. Terry, I wouldn't intentionally hurt you for the world. Still friends?"

"Sure. That doesn't mean I don't hope he goes away...permanently. Sorry about that."

Karyn sighed as she hung up the phone. There was a decency in Terry that made it impossible for her to want to intentionally hurt him. *What a mystery love is. Why is it so selective?* She thought about the day with Eric, and was unwilling to submit to sleep until the last memory had been thoroughly savored.

❖ ❖ ❖

It was a perfect Colorado day when Karyn drove up to the entrance of the Holiday Inn at nine-thirty in the morning.

"Do you mind if I drive?" asked Eric. "I haven't been behind the wheel of a car since the accident."

Karyn directed the route they took along the foothills. Purple mountains ascended in the distance, each range of peaks receding in the hazy atmosphere, with the furtherest peaks reaching up to meet an azure blue sky. An occasional puffy white cloud floated lazily on the horizon.

Driving through the entrance of the Big Thompson Canyon, Eric remarked, "No wonder they call this the Narrows, and the flood was such a tragedy. When I see this narrow canyon with it's vertical rock walls from ground level, it is terrifying to think of thirty feet of water coming down in such a short period of time."

"Yes. Thirty-four feet of the one-hundred-twenty feet of the floor of the canyon was eroded away by the force of the water. Take a look at that huge water pipe overhead. The original one was ripped out of the mountain, hit a house, and swept the house downstream with it."

"It's hard to imagine that kind of damage," said Eric, shaking his head as he viewed the terrain.

As the canyon widened, the destruction was still evident. A barren, silt-filled riverbed marked the area where oaks, willows, and aspen had stood. The water line was still clearly visible on the rocks and trees still standing. Much of the debris had been cleared away, but a few of the partially destroyed buildings were still boarded up.

They pulled off the side of the road near Drake, and got out to view the broad channel created by the flood. Huge boulders stood where they were thrown by the force of the water. Silt marked the place where the force of the water widened river channels and rushed down the mountain. Majestic pines stood scarred from the abrasion of objects floating downstream. Some of the remaining buildings showed the effects of water damage, some too structurally weakened to be repaired. Others had been renovated to conceal their previous condition. They both stood in silent awe as they considered what had happened on that night. It still seemed like a rerun of a TV disaster movie in which they had played varied roles.

Deep in thought, each with vivid memories of that night, they stood viewing the scene.

"I don't know what I intended to accomplish by suggesting we come, but this is something I'll never forget. The death and destruction reminds me of how close I came to death when I ejected from the plane. My worst nightmare was crashing over hostile waters. I've often wondered what would have happened if the fishermen had turned me into the KGB and accused me of spying. I'll never understand why they didn't. Instead, they helped me get back to a neutral zone."

Standing by the riverbed, Eric's thoughts returned to the present, and he reached out to put his arm around Karyn. "I guess life seems a little more precious to me because of what happened. Just think, if the flood had never happened, I wonder if we'd ever have met again." He looked deep into her eyes. "Do you believe in fate?"

Karyn thought a moment before she replied, "Not fate because fate has only questions, but no answers. I believe God has a divine plan for our lives. I don't understand why this tragedy took so many lives, and yet, you and I can say that it brought something special into our lives. Does that make sense?"

"I know God had something to do with the very fact that I'm alive. I made some pretty serious decisions while I was lying in that hospital bed. One of the military chaplains came to visit me during that time. He asked me if I was prepared to meet the Lord when I was floating around in the ocean after my plane went down. I told him my family had never been very religious. I'd never given it much thought until it looked like I might not make it. Some of the guys in the service talked about religion, but didn't live any differently when faced with tough choices. There was something different about that chaplain. He explained to me how I could have a personal relationship with the Lord. Since that time, I've actually started reading the Bible he gave me. There is so much in it that I don't understand. How did your parents feel about religion?"

"My parents have always attended a Bible teaching church. Corrine and I went to Sunday school every Sunday and church while we were home. I've really neglected doing so since I've been here. Cindy and I have managed to go to church on Easter Sunday, Christmas Eve, and some special occasions. I'm afraid that since I've been away from home, my relationship with the Lord hasn't been what it used to be. Since Jim's funeral, I've found a church where I feel at home."

Karyn smiled and continued, "We are really feeling philosophical this morning. I understand what you're saying, though. Death had really never touched me until I experienced the personal loss of someone I knew who was as young as Jim. That was bad enough, but when I saw how many families it affected at the rescue center, I suddenly felt very vulnerable. That's when I began to feel that I'd better begin to take my relationship with the Lord more seriously."

Slowly they walked up the road to the car, each deep in thought.

Pausing, Eric said, "What's the name of the church you've been attending."

"Faith Bible Church. Would you like to go this Sunday?"

"Sure." Taking her hand, he said, "There's no better time than the present if we're serious about this."

"You'll like Pastor Moore and Marty."

Karyn couldn't stop thinking about what Eric had said. She realized with a sense of guilt that she had never talked to him about the Lord or her spiritual values. Had she been afraid to trust the Lord regarding the feelings she had about Eric? As a teenager, she had always had strong convictions about becoming seriously involved with someone who made no claims of being a Christian. *What has happened to those values since I moved to Colorado? Am I just more concerned about having a good time and the freedom to make my own choices?*

✦ ✦ ✦

Vacationers strolled along Elkhorn Avenue, the main street of Estes Park, ducking into shops for treasured purchases or some tempting food item. Cars slowly moved along, allowing pedestrians to make their way across the busy street. Among the happy shoppers, occasional overseas visitors could be heard speaking a language not commonly heard in the area.

Laughing together, Eric and Karyn wandered in and out of the small boutiques. In the candy store, they teased each other about whether chocolate or brown sugar fudge was best. Eric spent more time looking at Karyn than he did looking in the windows. Her animated response to everything around them doubled the pleasure for him.

Passing a T-shirt shop, Karyn eyed a black T-shirt with Estes Park in gold letters and gilded with mountains in the background.

"I have to have that T-shirt," Karyn said, as she started to the entrance of the store.

Fingering through the racks, they found one identical to the window display in Karyn's size. Finding that, Karyn started for the men's sizes.

"Let's see if there's a matching one for you," she said, holding up a shirt for Eric's inspection. Pleased with her selection, Karyn insisted on making the purchase, despite Eric's objections.

Eric eyed the silver and turquoise belt buckles when they passed the silver jewelry displays in the window. "I've been looking for one like that," he said, pointing out a buckle with coral and turquoise inlay. "That's what I need for the western hat and jeans I bought the other day. Let's get the buckle and find a good place to eat our picnic. I'm starved."

While Eric made his purchase, Karyn browsed at the showcases of fine jewelry. When it seemed it was taking longer than necessary for Eric to make his purchase, Karyn walked back to the register where the clerk was ringing up the total on the cash register. Karyn was surprised at the amount.

Outside the store, Eric took a small box from his package. When he opened it, he pulled out a small gold chain with a heart-shaped charm, engraved with Estes Park in the center.

"Hold out your arm so I can put this on. This is just to remind you not to forget me while I'm gone," said Eric with a teasing smile. Karyn looked into his eyes and quietly said, "As if I could."

❖ ❖ ❖

The picnic area west of Estes, wooded with evergreens and quaking aspen, bordered an open meadow. Quietly surveying the beauty, Karyn mused, "It's great to come up here in the fall when the aspen are turning their spectacular gold. There are often elk out in those meadows. Then the road is lined with people taking pictures and watching the elk. The bulls, with their huge racks, will stand and bugle. It's such a strange high-pitched sound coming from such magnificent animals."

Karyn set out the fried chicken, potato salad, clam dip and bite-sized vegetables. Fruit beverages and brownies topped off the picnic menu. A hummingbird whizzed by, evidently attracted by the red flowers on the tablecloth. Chipmunks bravely approached them for any small morsel dropped or deliberately left for them.

❖ ❖ ❖

Eric looked at Karyn, her dark hair pulled back from her face and caught in a large barrette. White shorts were a sharp contrast to her sun-tanned legs as she leaned down to leave crumbs for a begging chipmunk. A green and white striped, sleeveless tank top curved gently over the bustline. Eric's heart swelled with pride as he looked at her. Suddenly he thought, *I really have no claim on her. What if she walks out of my life?*

❖ ❖ ❖

"Let's put this stuff away and take a walk. I want to see where this path leads to," Eric said. He started putting the food back into the picnic cooler.

Hand in hand, they started up the path which led up a gentle slope that gradually ascended around a steep rocky area. Slightly winded, they turned and gazed down at the view behind them.

"Isn't it beautiful?" Karyn commented.

Turning her around to face him, Eric replied, "You're beautiful. Not only outwardly, but you have those inner qualities that are so warm and appealing." He reached out to touch her soft, full lips with his forefinger while he cupped her chin in his other hand. "The women I meet are often shallow—like empty-headed mannequins." He pulled her into his arms. "Karyn, I love you, and I want to spend the rest of my life with you." Eric's heart was racing, and he could not stop its frantic beating. He had never said that to another woman. *What if she doesn't feel the same way about me?* It seemed an eternity before she replied. He felt robbed of air.

She reached up to place her arms around him. "I think I fell in love with you the day you rescued me on the mountain," she said, her voice full of wonder as she recalled the moment. "You were like a fairy tale fantasy. Your blond hair was blowing in the wind from the propeller blades, and your eyes looked as blue as the sky. The thing that impressed me most was your sensitive and caring attitude. I was terribly disappointed when I didn't hear from you. I was afraid to trust my own emotions for fear I might never see you again. When I tried to date other guys, I found myself comparing them to you, and there wasn't the same depth of emotion there. I always came home disappointed that it wasn't you."

His arms came out to encircle her, drawing her even closer. They stood there, clasped in each other's arms. Eric kissed her soundly, crushing her to him until she felt breathless. She wanted to feel his strong embrace the rest of her life.

❖ ❖ ❖

The relaxing days spent at the pool in the sun gave Eric a healthy tan. Swimming proved to be great therapy for his stiff limbs. He began to feel a renewed sense of good health.

"Tomorrow morning I have to report to Fitzsimmons for my medical checkup. They will probably give me some idea of what to expect about my future of flying."

"Are you worried about the outcome?" asked Karyn. She tried to read the inflection in Eric's voice.

"I'm beginning to feel like the accident never happened, but until they release me, I'm not sure."

Karyn wanted so much to reassure him, but realized she could say nothing that would take away the uncertainty. She reached out for his hand as a gesture of understanding. *I can appreciate the anxiety Eric must feel. I'm sure we both feel a degree of uncertainty about what the future holds. Lord, I know you want me to take it one day at a time, and allow You to work out Your perfect plan in our lives.*

✣ ✣ ✣

Karyn turned from her calculator to answer the phone on her desk.

"Karyn, how would you like to go for an airplane ride? The doctors just gave their okay for me to fly again." The exuberance in his voice was hard to miss. "They gave me another week of leave before I have to report back to base."

"Eric, that's wonderful. I could hardly wait to hear from you to know the outcome of your examination. I'd love to go flying, but right this minute? I'm in the middle of quarterly reports," she said, surveying the work on her desk.

"No, not today, but I'll make reservations for a couple of hours Saturday morning. I haven't flown a plane since my accident, and I'm dying to take one up just to see how it feels again," he said. He looked out at the bright morning sky from his hotel window. "Will that work out for you?"

"Perfect. It sounds like you're getting restless and ready to go back to flying." A hint of wistfulness crept into her voice.

"I'm anxious to get back to flying, but it will be hard to leave after spending this time with you."

"If I'm going to get out of the office by noon, I'd better finish these reports. Shall we pick up lunch at the deli to eat in the park before we swim?"

"Sounds good to me. I'll make the plane reservation and see you at noon. Love you."

❖ ❖ ❖

Eric stepped into the hanger that doubled as an office at Fort Collin's Airpark. The airport manager was on the radio, giving landing instructions to a Cessna circling the field. He looked up, nodding his head to acknowledge Eric.

"What can I do for you?"

"I reserved a Bonanza for a couple of hours this morning. Eric Johnson's the name."

"Okay, Johnson. The Bonanza just came back from her yearly inspection, so she should be in great shape," and he handed Eric the keys.

Karyn got out of the car and walked over to the plane as Eric started around the aircraft for a pre-flight check. Curious, she followed him around while he checked the nose gear, kicked the tires for proper inflation, and looked at the struts. Satisfied there was no damage to the aileron and flaps on the left, he proceeded to the right.

"I hate to show my ignorance, but do you have to do this for every plane you fly? I thought the mechanics took care of all those details."

"It's a precautionary measure to ensure maintenance people haven't missed anything. Hey, Beautiful, I have to look out for the precious cargo I'm taking up in this plane," he said, winking at Karyn.

After completing the circle check, he checked the oil and the surrounding area for leaks.

"Everything looks in good shape, " he said as he stepped up on the wing. Giving Karyn a hand up, he then climbed into the pilot's seat. Once she was seated, he turned to check her seat belt to see that it was secure. He smiled at her with obvious pleasure. After carefully covering the pre-flight run-up check on the instrument panel, he hollered "All clear" from the open window and started the engine.

At the run-up area, Karyn watched with interest as Eric's skillful hands completed the run-up check, and he turned to eye the surrounding area for other planes.

"Unacom B-56 south bound, departing on runway 11."

The engine thundered with full throttle as Eric pulled up the gear handle. Karyn's throat tightened while watching the airspeed indicator. Then came that moment when the vibrations stopped, and the plane lifted off the ground. Karyn could hear the engines roaring smoothly. The sensation of speed abated as the plane climbed effortlessly from the tarmac into the sky.

"I love the feeling of lift off," said Karyn. She looked over to see the smile of complete satisfaction on Eric's face.

They made a circle over Fort Collins and flew from north to south over Horsetooth Reservoir. Boats looked like toys on the seven-mile lake. South along the foothills, the ripening wheat fields and tilled soil ran in parallel patterns across the rolling hills. Housing developments, surrounded by trees, spread across the landscape in clusters to the east of Loveland. Farmland and pastures, green from early summer rains, lay in crazy-quilt patterns on the eastern plains between Loveland and Greeley. Following the course of the South Platte River to Fort Morgan, Eric turned north toward Cheyenne across the grasslands. An antelope herd, grazing on the hillside, spooked as Eric flew lower to get a closer look.

"Everything is so peaceful up here," commented Eric. "There's nothing like the exhilaration of flying in space. See that bird soaring over there. He has nothing on us," laughed Eric. He reached over to take Karyn's hand. "I wanted to share this passion of mine with you."

✤ ✤ ✤

Karyn rolled over to shut off the alarm, smiling with anticipation. Today, Eric was picking her up for the ten-thirty Sunday morning church service. They had agreed he would drive her car back to the Holiday Inn, and he would come by for her.

The church, a lovely, old historical brick building, was located not far from her condo.

Pastor Moore preached on the text," Eye hath not seen, nor the ear heard, the things that are prepared for those who love the Lord." He then expounded on the thirty-three promises the believer has in Christ.

Karyn turned to smile at Eric beside her, and squeezed his hand. *It's wonderful to know that we can both be the recipients of those promises!*

After the service, Pastor Moore and Marty stood at the door and greeted the families as they walked through the foyer

"Karyn, how nice to see you," he said, extending his hand.

Marty gave Karyn and Eric a warm smile. Addressing Eric, she said, "And I don't believe we've had the pleasure of meeting you."

"I'd like you to meet Eric Johnson," replied Karyn. "Eric's in the military. He's been on leave for a few weeks while he is recovering from an accident."

Marty, intrigued by the play of emotions across Karyn's expressive face, said, "We are so happy to have you visiting this morning. We trust Fort Collins has been an ideal place for a complete recovery."

"Yes, it has been." Eric turned to give Karyn a smile and a look that said more than words could say. He placed his hand at Karyn's back in a protective gesture to guide her to the door and down the steps from the church.

Marty looked at her husband and whispered, "What a nice young man. I hope they find happiness together."

"Honey, you're such an impossible matchmaker." He gave his wife a fond look, and turned to greet several couples who were leaving.

❖ ❖ ❖

All too soon to suit both of them, Eric's leave was over. At the airport, Eric pulled Karyn into his arms to say goodbye. All his emotions and longings went into that final kiss. He was flying back to California without a clear idea of what his next assignment would be.

❖ ❖ ❖

An overwhelming feeling of loneliness swept over Karyn. *Lord, I don't know what's in your plan for us, but please bring Eric safely back again.*

Chapter 22

The Wedding

E ric called frequently. Karyn lived for his overseas phone calls. She was always reluctant to hang up the phone and lose the sense of closeness she felt between them.

On a lazy Saturday afternoon, she stood in her living room looking out the window at the myriad marigolds and mums in the flowerbeds, still colorful even though it was mid-September. A slight breeze sent fallen leaves scuttling across the lawn. Tired from a busy work schedule, yet feeling as restless as the leaves on the lawn, Karyn wandered about the room, not really seeing anything. *How long will it be before I see Eric again?*

To break the sense of boredom, she decided to stir up a batch of fudge brownies. Just as she began to assemble the ingredients, the phone rang.

"Guess what?" Eric said when she picked up the phone. The animation in his voice drew her immediate attention. "Since I passed my physical, I put in a transfer for Denver and have to report at Lowry Air Force Base by the last of September. How would you like to marry this fly-boy in October?"

"I can't take that many surprises all at once!" Karyn said, as she rapidly tried to comprehend what he was saying. Eric laughed, the sound coming across the wire rolling time backwards. He had a wonderful laugh she recalled. She had heard it frequently on their rafting trip and on the ski slope.

"I said, let's get married when I get to Denver. I can't stand this bachelor life any longer." His jovial and teasing manner changed to soft and tender words that sounded almost like a caress. "Karyn, I love you, and I've missed you so."

"Oh, sweetheart, I've missed you too, and I'd marry you in a minute…but my parents are the old fashioned kind. They will want to meet my prospective husband, or they would never forgive me. Besides, I want to show you off to my family and friends. Do you think you can wait long enough to do that?"

"I'm a reasonable man, even if an impatient one. When can we set the date? Would a Christmas wedding give you enough time?"

"I've dreamed of a Christmas wedding, but maybe we should talk about this some more when you get here. Okay?"

"Am I to take that as a yes? If so, maybe I can be patient that long." He breathed a long sigh into the phone.

"That's a definite yes about marrying you. And maybe about the date," she said, smiling into the phone.

"Seriously, I'll let you know later about my exact arrival time. Meet me at the airport, and we'll go out and celebrate. Darling, you've just made me the happiest man in the Air Force!"

Karyn hung up the phone, wondering if she had dreamed it all. The conversation went on in her mind for minutes to follow.

I have to call Cindy, and tell her the news.

When Cindy picked up the phone, Karyn got right to the point. "How would you like to be my maid of honor? Eric just proposed to me from California." Karyn's voice was exuberant.

"It's a little unconventional, isn't it? I haven't seen enough of him to know if I approve," she said, laughingly. "I know you haven't been the same since you met him last summer. He really must be something, considering all the other dates you've turned down. Seriously, you know I'd love to be your maid of honor, but you do have to promise to throw me your bouquet."

"Maybe you can catch Mark, along with the bouquet," teased Karyn.

Smiling, she dialed home. Her mother answered the phone. "Karyn! I'm surprised to hear from you again so soon after talking to you over the weekend. Is everything okay?"

"Mom, how would you like to help me plan a Christmas wedding?"

"Not on your life! I always said that I would never have one of my daughters getting married during the Christmas holiday. Has your young pilot lost his mind?"

"Oh, Mother, I'm serious. He's being transferred to Denver as soon as the paperwork goes through. In the meantime, he'll have some leave the first of October. I want you and Dad to meet him then. You're overdue for a visit here, anyway."

✦ ✦ ✦

Eric stepped from the plane looking tan and healthy, moving with the natural grace of a man raised outdoors. Karyn rushed into his arms, a sense of pride and possessiveness engulfing her. She watched his eyes light up with that exclusive look that made her feel she was the most important person in the world to him.

"Would you like me to drive?" he asked when they reached the parking garage. Taking the keys from Karyn's outstretched hand, he slid into the driver's seat. Easing the car out of the congestion of the terminal traffic, Eric reached over for Karyn's hand. "I made reservations at Brittany Hill for dinner. According to Colorado time, we should just beat the crowd for the evening dinner hour. Sound good to you?"

Brittany Hill, with its quaint little inn atmosphere, was a perfect place for a quiet, romantic dinner. They ordered strawberry daiquiris while they waited for the main course.

"Now, let's talk about plans for Christmas. Did my prospective in-laws approve...of course, contingent on our meeting prior to that?"

"My mother has always said she would never allow her daughters to have a wedding over the Christmas holiday. Now, unless you can persuade her otherwise, we might have to set a later date." Karyn's eyes danced with mischief.

"In that case, we could elope. Did you tell her I'm an impatient guy? Maybe we could get married the day after Christmas. Seriously, my parents plan to come to Colorado in a couple of weeks. If your parents could fly out from Chicago at that time, you and I could host an engagement dinner then."

"That would be wonderful! We could make out our guest lists and take care of some of the details while they're here."

The entrée of steak and lobster was superb, and their waiter hovered over them to take care of their every wish.

Karyn and Eric locked eyes across the table. She looked at the face of the man she loved, his blue eyes, blond, wavy hair, straight aristocratic nose, and well formed lips. She could honestly say there was nothing about him she didn't find attractive.

Their conversation bubbled with enthusiasm as they discussed tentative wedding plans. The excitement of being together escalated as they finished dinner and walked to the car holding hands.

They barely noticed the miles as they drove north on I-25 out of the suburbs of Denver.

"I want you to meet my brother Matt. Of course, he will be my best man, and by that time, one of my flying buddies, Rod, should be back in the States."

"I've already asked Corrine and Cathy to be my bridesmaids, and Cindy my maid of honor. I called Cindy right after you proposed because I couldn't wait to tell her. She thinks I'm a bit unconventional," laughed Karyn, "but she can't wait for the big day to catch my bridal bouquet."

At the Loveland exit, Eric turned off the interstate.

"Are you taking the scenic route to Fort Collins?" she asked.

"Yes. It's a beautiful, moonlit night, and I thought we might drive up the canyon."

A full moon hovered over the eastern horizon. It's surface turned platinum as it climbed toward the mountains to the west, lighting a path as Eric drove into the lower canyon. Stars twinkled like diamonds strewn across the clear night sky.

"It's a beautiful night, isn't it?" commented Karyn, as she surveyed the night sky around her. Weaving her fingers through Eric's, she snuggled up close to him. Her world felt complete.

Eric drove leisurely up the canyon road until he came to a place where the road leveled out. Pulling the car over to a turnout, he shut off the motor. His voice held a serious note as he said, "This will always be a special place to me. It was here in the midst of all the chaos that I saw you again and began to realize what it means to truly love someone." Turning on the overhead light, Eric handed her a little wooden box, resembling a miniature treasure chest. When she lifted the lid, she found a velvet-covered jeweler's box inside.

Eric took the small box and opened it to remove a sparkling solitaire diamond in a unique designer mounting. Taking Karyn's hand to slip the ring on her finger, he said, "You have given me the most precious gift you could give me...your love." And he kissed her with all the passion of young love.

Each time Eric left, Karyn found it harder and harder to say goodbye. Even though he would soon be stationed in Denver, she knew his mission could take him out of the U.S. The knowledge that she would soon see him again motivated her to throw all her energy into making plans for their wedding. They hadn't talked about what she would do about her job, completing her master's degree, or where they would live.

When Eric returned to Beale Air Force Base in California, he called to say, "My parents asked when to make plane reservations for our engagement party. Where do we want to have it, and how many people do we want to invite?"

"The Hermitage Inn would be a nice place to have it, depending on the number of guests. Let's keep it small and intimate, shall we? We can include everyone in the wedding."

"Good idea. I've checked with my commanding officer to make sure I can get time off. He said that would be no problem. Let me know when you talk to your folks. Love you, Sweetheart."

✤ ✤ ✤

Eric met his parents at Stapleton on the second of October. They rented a car at the airport, and arrived in Fort Collins in time to shower and change for dinner.

Karyn's parents had arrived several days earlier to spend time with their daughter. Mrs. Anderson and Karyn busily compiled a wedding guest list and did some preliminary shopping to look at bridal gowns and bridesmaid dresses in Denver.

Since her father had no desire to shop with the ladies, he decided to check out the golf courses in Fort Collins.

Karyn and her parents agreed to meet Eric and his parents in the lounge at the Marriott. Eric and Karyn made the introductions to the family members.

"I thought it would be nice to meet here so you could see where we plan to have the wedding reception. We've already made reservations for December 20th. The staff just needs the approximate number of guests attending."

"Now that we have taken care of that, we'd better hurry so as not to be late at the Hermitage Inn," said Eric. "Karyn's friends will be there soon."

"Mr. and Mrs. Johnson can ride with us if you young people want to go together," suggested Mr. Anderson.

"Thank you, sir," said Eric, as he patted the shoulder of the older man who was soon to become his father-in-law.

Karyn was touched as she watched her dad's warm response to the man she loved.

Once in the car, turning to Karyn, Eric confided, "I'm so glad we've had a minute to talk before we get there. Honey, I hope my parents will be on their good behavior this evening. They like to drink a little too much, and sometimes they get carried away on special occasions. I don't want them to embarrass you or your family."

"Whatever happens, darling, we won't let it spoil this evening for us. Okay? If they are going to be my in-laws, I have to accept them as they are. Maybe that's something you and I will just have to pray about."

Eric helped Karyn out of the car at the Inn. Lifting a box out of the back seat, he turned to her and pinned a gardenia corsage on her midnight-blue silk dress.

"How did you know that was my favorite corsage?" exclaimed Karyn, breathing in the delicate fragrance of the flowers.

"I think you told me that at some point in our conversations. I intentionally made note of that information to use at some future date, and this seems to be the appropriate occasion." Then, he leaned down to touch Karyn's soft lips with a lingering kiss.

Cindy, Mark, Cathy and Dave arrived as Karyn and Eric opened the door to enter the Inn. Wade and Helen were seated in the lounge when the rest of the dinner party walked in.

Taking Eric's hand while the group gathered around, Karyn said, " I want you to meet my fiance, Eric Johnson." Her radiating glow was impossible to miss.

"Eric, I began to wonder if I was ever going to get to see you again," laughed Cindy. "Karyn kept talking about you, but I was almost convinced that you were a figment of her imagination."

"We're going to change that," said Eric, as he put his arm around Karyn and gave her a smile that dispelled any doubts about the future.

"It's impossible to miss...these two are in love," laughed Cindy, making a sweeping gesture to the rest of the group.

Once seated, Mr. and Mrs. Johnson ordered drinks as soon as the cocktail waitress came to take orders.

Eric gave Karyn a questioning look, and she returned the look with a smile that eased the tension he was feeling.

"I have a little gift for you, Karyn," said Eric's mother, as she handed Karyn a beautifully wrapped package.

"Shall I open it now or later?" asked Karyn, looking across the table at Mrs. Johnson.

"I think it would be nice if you opened it now."

Karyn opened the box , which contained a photo album filled with pictures of Eric from infancy to the present. He looked handsome dressed in his Air Force uniform.

"Oh, what a lovely gift," exclaimed Karyn, beginning to turn the pages. She laughed as she saw what must have been Eric's first grade school picture. "What a cute little boy you were," she said, turning to see Eric smiling with amusement as he looked at the photo.

"I've also included some pages that trace our genealogy back to our Norwegian ancestors," said Eric's mother with a look of pride.

"With a history like that, what else would they have named me besides Eric," he teased, while everyone laughed at the humor.

The waiter interrupted the conversation when he came in with a huge tray to start serving dinner.

Much to Eric's relief, the evening went smoothly, and he could tell his parents were using unusual restraint.

Following dessert and coffee, the well-wishers rose to leave. Wade extended his hand to Eric saying, "I hope you know what a lucky man you are. This little lady is pretty special to us. Congratulations to both of you."

"Eric, now that we've met again, I have to say that I'm not sure who is the luckier, Karyn for having you or you for having Karyn," said Cindy as she and Mark lingered to offer their warmest wishes. "Whichever is the case, we must get together again before you have to leave."

"Why don't you give us a call, and we'll arrange to meet you and Mark at the Charco Broiler one night this week," said Karyn.

"That would be fun," said Cindy, looking to Mark for confirmation.

"We'll take the Johnsons back to their motel, and meet you at the condo later," said Mr. Anderson to Karyn. The older couples said their good-byes to the other guests and started toward the door.

Karyn smiled appreciatively. Thanks, Dad," as she gave him a kiss on the cheek for his thoughtfulness. Turning to Eric, she said, "Would you like to get together for breakfast in the morning?"

"That's a great idea," said Eric. "We could meet you and your parents about eight o'clock in the coffee shop. Okay, Mom?"

Everyone nodded in agreement. Eric turned to his parents with a smile. "Don't wait up for me," he said, as he and Karyn started for her car. Their parents laughed as they made their way across the parking lot.

❖ ❖ ❖

Karyn switched on the lights in her condo, and put on one of her favorite records.

Leading her to the sofa and pulling her close beside him, Eric said, "We need this time to make some plans. Where do you think we should live since I'm going to be stationed in Denver? You still have your job here, and you will have classes until graduation in the spring."

"Would you object to commuting back and forth?" asked Karyn. "The rent will be cheaper here than around the base," she said with a twinkle in her eye.

"I would rather live here than in Denver," said Eric, "and no, I don't mind commuting. We won't know for a while how much time I may be gone. It seems logical to live here. Besides, this place is pretty special because you're here," he said, wrapping her tightly in his arms as he turned to kiss her.

Releasing her, he continued, "We need to consider what you want to do after graduation, too. What are your thoughts about that?"

"I've had my application in for two years to teach art at Rocky Mountain High School. There is such a long waiting list for the foothills area. How that turns out might determine where we want to be for the next couple of years."

"You know we can't stay here forever. There's no room for the kids," said Eric, looking into Karyn's eyes.

Before Eric had a chance to continue, Karyn's parents walked in the door. "It's beginning to feel like winter out there," said Mrs. Anderson, as she hung her coat in the hall closet.

"If you two young people will excuse us, " said Mr. Anderson, "we're going to bed. Shopping and golf games are beginning to wear us out." With a chuckle, he and Mrs. Anderson started toward the hall.

"Karyn, we feel bad about putting you out of your room. We really could have gotten a motel," said her mother, stepping back into the living room.

"Mom, don't even think about it. I love having you and dad here. Eric and I were just saying that someday we might need a larger house." An intimate smile passed between the two as they considered the future.

Mr. and Mrs. Anderson closed the bedroom door, leaving Karyn and Eric to continue their discussion.

"Now another very important topic we haven't discussed is, where are we going to spend our honeymoon?" asked Eric. "I will have three week's leave."

"Let's spend the first few days in the mountains, shall we?"

asked Karyn, her eyes dancing.

"My folks have offered to give us a cruise to the Bahamas for a wedding gift. What do you think?"

"How lovely of them!" exclaimed Karyn, her face aglow.

"However, I love the idea of having you all to myself for the first few days before I have to share you with anyone else," said Eric, enclosing her tightly in his arms.

❖ ❖ ❖

The soloist sang "Oh, Promise Me" as Karyn and her bridesmaids walked down the hall toward the foyer. Corinne's twins stared at her in awe when she came through the door of the foyer.

In her miniature bridal gown, her eyes glowing, Lindsey said, "Aunt Karyn, you and I are twins! I get to throw the petals all the way up to the front of the church."

Not to be outdone, Larry piped up, "But my job is really important because I'm carrying the rings."

Leaning over to smile at them, Karyn said, "This is a very happy day for Aunt Karyn, and I'm so glad that both of you can have an important part in the wedding."

To the sounds of Mendelsshon's Wedding March, the bridal party started down the isle. Karyn followed the attendants, with her hand tucked into the crook of her father's arm.

Catching the reflection of the candlelit aisle, her fitted white satin gown glittered with sequins and little seed pearls. A waist-length tulle veil, caught in a satin headband, bordered with sequins and pearls, cast a halo around Karyn's dark hair.

Evergreen boughs with white candles and burgundy velvet bows graced the end of each pew in the quaint little stone church.

Radiant with anticipation, Karyn looked at Eric, standing tall and at ease beside the alter, smiling as he watched her walk toward him.

An arch of evergreen boughs with white poinsettias, burgundy velvet bows, and giant candelabra made a holiday backdrop for the bridesmaids in their burgundy velvet gowns.

Eric's brother Matt, Corrine's husband, Randy, and Eric's pilot friend, Rod, stood beside him in their black tuxedos, with white shirts and burgundy cummerbunds.

As her father released Karyn, and Eric took her hand, Karyn realized this was the man to whom she was entrusting her entire future—and she had no reservations about that decision!

They exchanged their vows under an arch, aromatic with the fragrance of pine. With her hand in his, they repeated the vows, which were ages old, yet ever new, as they pledged their lasting love to each other.

Karyn and Eric, filled with awe at the solemn commitment they were making to each other, could see the love reflected in each other's eyes.

"God has given each of you the incredible gift of love," said Karyn's own pastor from Chicago, who had flown out for the wedding. "Love is like a lovely delicate rose, which needs to be handled carefully. If gently cared for, it emits a fragrance to all around. The stem is strong, yet there are a few thorns. To enjoy the beauty, you must be prepared to suffer a few pricks now and then.

"The beauty of a Christian marriage is that you never need to walk alone. God is always there beside you to guide you over the rough spots. If you always remember that, you will have a marriage that is not only a beautiful relationship, but also an honor to Him."

The pastor returned to his seat, and the soloist sang "O Perfect Love."

❖ ❖ ❖

The reception at the Marriott was festive with family and friends. As Eric and Karyn cut the cake, and shared the wedding toast, Cindy said to Corrine,

"Those two make me so envious!"

That's the kind of relationship I want. I've never seen a couple who seems so happy and right for each other.

Karyn and Eric circulated among their friends and family, as the photographer busily took shots of the milling guests.

Mike and Julie came up to congratulate the euphoric couple. Julie hugged Karyn and very quietly said, "What a lucky girl you are. I think you've made a wonderful choice." And to the two of them, "You must bring Eric up to the cabin so we can get better acquainted."

Jake walked around the well-wishers to shake Eric's hand, saying, "You take care of this little gal, or you'll have to answer to me. Of course, I guess I should take into consideration, you were the one who rescued her in the first place. Seriously, Jill and I wish the two of you the best."

On a silent signal to his brother, Eric took Karyn's hand and they quietly left the reception room. Matt and Cindy proceeded to the front door, where Karyn's car stood decorated with white streamers, a trail of tin cans, and "Just Married" signs on the windows. Matt and Cindy appeared to be waiting for the newlyweds.

Guests gathered with their rice to shower the departing couple. College friends, who had planned in detail how to stall the newlyweds, waited impatiently to implement their plan.

Karyn and Eric quickly slipped into their rooms to change into their travel clothes. Giggling like two conspirators, they ran down the hall to a back exit, and slipped out to get into Eric's new midnight-blue Riviera waiting in the rear parking lot.

Cathy and Rod ran out of a side door and climbed into the back seat of Karyn's car while alerted college friends stood watching. When they realized the switch, they pelted Cathy and Rod with rice just for the fun of it. Matt squealed out of the parking lot with tin cans trailing noisily behind. Cindy, Matt, Rod, and Cathy were laughing hilariously as they watched a trail of cars begin to follow them out onto Horsetooth road.

"Won't they be surprised to find out Eric and Karyn are already gone," laughed Matt, as they watched the cars giving chase.

❖ ❖ ❖

It was spitting snow when Eric and Karyn drove up Big Thompson Canyon to Estes. Feathery flakes began blanketing the earth in a fluffy layer of white. Eric drove up to the entrance of Timberlane Lodge to check in. They looked forward to spending the first few days of their honeymoon in a secluded little cabin, surrounded by the mountains they both loved.

The log cabin was aglow with blinking white lights as Eric parked the car. Lights trailed around the eaves and porch rail, and more lights were strung around the snow-tipped evergreens flanking the small porch.

"Oh, how lovely," exclaimed Karyn as she viewed the lights and the bright red door, hung with a traditional Christmas wreath. "It's so perfect."

"I thought you'd be pleased, " said Eric, as he smiled with pleasure at her response. Stepping out of the car, they began collecting their luggage from the trunk and car seat. Tramping through the fluffy snow, they laughed with abandon as they reached the porch of the cabin. Eric turned at the door and set down the luggage he was carrying. He took Karyn's makeup case and her clothing bag from her hand and placed them with the luggage. Then he picked her up in his arms. She was dusted with snowflakes and laughing with sheer joy as she placed a little kiss on Eric's cold nose.

"Since I have this beautiful bundle in my arms, you'll have to open the door. I can't find the knob," laughed Eric.

A fire burned in the fireplace as they opened the door of the small modern cottage. Complimentary champagne chilled in a bucket, and a basket of cheese, crackers and fruit was placed on the coffee table. Red and white poinsettias graced each side of the fireplace and a wooden bowl filled with nuts sat on an end table.

"It's all so lovely!" exclaimed Karyn, as Eric put her down. Her eyes danced with laughter as she did a pirouette in the center of the room.

Pulling her into his arms, Eric possessively planted a passionate kiss on the mouth of his new bride and felt her molding to his body. The warmth of her body filled his senses. As the light from the fireplace played on her face, Eric breathed, "I thank God every day that He brought you into my life."

The snow fell gently around the cabin, creating a silent, white world outside. Inside, two people in love shared their dreams and their lives with each other.

Bibliography

The Big Thompson DISASTER.
A collection of editorial and pictorial material concerning Colorado's tragic flash flood of July 31, 1976.
Published by Lithographic Press, Loveland, Colorado.

The Big Thompson Flood. July 31, 1976
Published by C. F. Boone, 1976. Edited by Don Cotton.

BIG THOMPSON: Profile of a Natural Disaster
by David McComb
Pruett Publishing Company, Boulder Colorado.

Oral Interview: Big Thompson Flood
Margaret Batie, Marie Faust, Doris Wells, Patricia Schumacher

Flood Commission Manual

Local newspaper accounts

SR-71 Revealed
by Richard H. Graham, Col. USAF (Ret)

About the Author

Bertie, a native Coloradoan, and her husband, Russell, live near the majestic Rocky Mountains. She attended Colorado State University.

She and her pastor-husband served in churches in Colorado, Nebraska, and Wyoming until retirement. She was actively involved in Christian Women's Clubs in several capacities, including Chairman for two years.

Following her research on the devastation of the Big Thompson flood, the drama touched a responsive cord within the writer to want to share that tragedy in a fictional setting.

In between working on this project and a follow-up novel, she finds time to travel and visit with her three daughters and families, including six grandchildren.

For all readers who loved

TERROR Before the Dawn

by Bertie Woodward

CIRCLE OF LOVE

Doors bang!
Emergency personal rush a small helpless infant
to surgery in order to save it's life.
Dr. Mark Preston is involved in caring for the baby,
whose life hangs in the balance by a fragile thread.
Cindy witnesses the intense drama from the
waiting room of McKee Hospital as
Dr. Mark oversees the delicate operation.
What happens to Cindy's relationship
to Dr. Mark Preston?

*Will their love survive the strains
of a three-circle relationship?*

Karyn and Eric face their own challenges
as Eric continues to fly dangerous missions.
Their friendship with Mark and Cindy is strengthened
as they support them in a commitment that
is "beyond the call of duty."

COMING OUT IN THE SPRING OF 2002

TERROR
Before the Dawn by Bertie Woodward

TO ORDER ADDITIONAL COPIES OF THIS BOOK PLEASE USE THIS

ORDER FORM

SEND TO:

NAME _____

ADDRESS _____

_____

CITY_____ STATE _____ ZIP_____

Daytime Phone#_____

SEND ADDITIONAL COPIES TO:

NAME _____

ADDRESS _____

_____

CITY_____ STATE _____ ZIP_____

Daytime Phone#_____

**PLEASE MAKE CHECKS
PAYABLE TO:**
Twin Star Publishing
3200 Sumac Street
Fort Collins, CO 80526

**ALLOW 4-6 WEEKS
FOR DELIVERY**

This offer is subject to change
without notice.

QUANTITY	Book Sale Totals
_____ @ **$12.95 each =**	_____
Sales Tax	_____
Sub Total	_____
Shipping & Handling	_____
$1.50 first book	
$1.00 each additional	
TOTAL SALE	_____